Children of the Diadems

Sonia Braithwaite

Book Two

Mephisto's Plots

This book is a work of fiction: Due to the broad spiritual elements in this story, I have randomly referenced Jesus, his disciples, and other gods and goddesses, from other cultural beliefs and practices, none of which are intended as a blight or disrespect to their characters, past or present. I have chosen to use these elements, as praise and recognition of the richly diverse cultural heritage, in which I feel privileged to be able to be a part of.

Published 29/04/2014

Book cover illustrated by Matthew Willis

ISBN: 9780957274037

Dedication:

To my granddaughter Yemaya

Chapter One

The Festive Season

It was the month of December, and the weeks leading up to the Christmas holiday were always a very busy, but fun time at St Catharine's Primary School. It was especially so for Tom, because it was the turn of Year 6 to put on a show to be remembered, and he was passionate about acting.

Most of the pupils were on their best behaviour while they prepared for the end-of-year concert. As was customary, the children in their final year had to perform to the whole school, in front of visiting parents, relatives, friends, and all the teachers. This year, even the local newspaper had been sent an invitation and had accepted. Those pupils from Class 5 who had offered to help on-set and with other preparations, like dressing and decorating the school, to help give it a true festive look, using the many donated Christmas decorations, were excused from their lessons at those times, and, like Tom, they too appeared to be cheerful, they joked and laughed happily while they worked.

This particular year, the theme was most unusual, it was titled, 'Divinity.'

Year 6 had chosen to stage a musical about Mary's son, Jesus.

Acting or anything to do with public speaking wasn't really one of Carl's favourite subjects, his face grew sour at the very thought of taking part. He walked around with a most serious expression, which none of his friends had ever seen him take on before.

Mrs Maureen Trench, the drama teacher in charge, had auditioned and given parts to various pupils. Carl looked miserable during rehearsal because he had been the last to put his hand up for a part, so he had no choice. The teacher had thought there was only one character left to place, and that was the main character, Jesus. Carl was upset about the part he was given, as he didn't feel he was the right person to play the lead role, and so he complained.

"From this day on, I hate school and I hate Christmas! Me, to act as *Jesus* - Is she kidding me? I can't play that part."

He spent a whole week walking around offering bribes and begging others to change roles with him, but even his best friend, Tom, said no to him. Craig was the last person Carl asked, and he eagerly agreed, so they approached the teacher about swapping.

"No, sorry Carl, but Craig begged for the part he has. And not only that, I personally think the role of Jesus suits you more than it suits him."

"*You* might think so, Miss," was Tom's sympathetic response in support of his friend.

"Why do you think that I am right to play the part of Jesus, Miss?" Carl asked one day during rehearsal.

Mrs Trench replied that she couldn't think of anyone it would suit better, as she believed Jesus' complexion was more like Carl's than Craig's.

"Well," protested Carl, looking very unhappy, "he wasn't black either."

"Well, Carl," the teacher replied, "since you put it so bluntly, I believe that Jesus was more black than white."

"No Miss, he wasn't," insisted Craig, who had walked up and placed himself between Tom and Carl. "I have a picture of him in my room."

"How sweet," teased Sean Sculley, "Hey, listen up every one, did you hear that? Craig has a picture of Jesus, hanging in his bedroom." Sean grinned deliberately.

Everyone except the teacher, Tom and Carl, giggled, but Craig didn't seem to care, he looked defiant.

"Yeah, we have a lover of the god man in our class," taunted Stanley Baker. "Craig has a picture of the Christ, the man himself. Is it remarkable or isn't it?" He persisted, looking around the classroom, with the same kind of troublesome grin as Sean's. Some of the pupils laughed at his sarcasm, but others pointed mockingly at him.

"Don't laugh, it's not funny, *I have*," said Craig, in what might have been the most impressive accent he had ever used. "I'll bring it tomorrow and show all of you, since none of you believe me. Seriously," he added with conviction, "Jesus, he was a white man, with blond hair and blue eyes."

"I bet he looks just like you Crageous?" teased Stanley. Everyone laughed again, even the teacher looked amused.

"You can all laugh, I don't care," Craig responded boldly. "You won't laugh tomorrow when I show you the picture. I'll have the last laugh then."

"Aren't you forgetting something Craig? I've seen the picture you have, and someone posed for it, numbskull," remarked Nikhil.

4

"As much as I do believe that you might be right, Nikhil Gupta," said the teacher, sounding a little firm, "You have just used a term that is deliberately insulting to Craig's intelligence. I will not tolerate the use of offensive words in this class. You will apologise to Craig Brackenridge this instant."

"OK then, sorry Miss, sorry Craig," muttered Nikhil, unconvincingly.

Looking a little displeased, the teacher continued, "Now, the point Nikhil just mentioned about the picture. I have heard that it was a painter named Leonardo Da Vinci, who painted the portrait of Jesus. Have any of you heard of this particular artist?" The entire class shook their heads. The teacher looked surprised. "It would appear that Da Vinci had a very versatile mind," she continued, "He was not only good at painting, he sculpted and designed too."

"Gee whiz, golly, all those jobs at once," said Naomi Jones. The teacher looked at Naomi pleasantly, and then Carl grumbled.

"That changes nothing. Jesus was a Jew and I am not a Jew."

"That makes no difference," commented Mrs Trench, casually. "In those days, I believe that Jews were mostly brown in complexion."

"So," replied Carl, sounding disappointed, realising he was fighting a losing battle, "This is just a pretend show." He ended in a huff.

"That's another good reason why you should play the part," said the teacher.

Carl stepped aside, he went quiet. He realised that no matter what argument he put forward, he was lumbered with playing the role, as Jesus.

Finally, he announced miserably, "Oh alright then, I'll do it Miss, but not because I want to. It's because I have no other option, I'm being forced."

"Good, Carl," said Mrs Trench, in a gentle manner. She had ignored his last comments and his sulks. Carl looked surprised by the teacher's calm response. The rest of the group smiled at him, but he didn't smile back, he looked really disappointed.

Craig had asked to be included in as many singing parts as possible, and he was, even though his singing voice wasn't up to standard, as was clear during the audition. He had also been given the role of King Herod, who was supposed to have been a cruel king.

Sean, accepted the role, as Peter, the disciple who

denied knowing Jesus, and Luke Reid gladly agreed to act as Judas, the disciple who was paid to point Jesus out to the Roman soldiers. Luke clapped his hands and cheered and smiled happily, when the teacher made the announcement.

Nikhil had asked for the part of Joseph of Arimathea, a rich Jew who some people believed might have been a relative of Jesus. Nikhil got his wish and looked satisfied.

Tom bravely accepted to act as Pontius Pilate and was booed, but he didn't seem to care, even though he had read earlier that it was Pilate who had ordered Jesus' execution by hanging on a cross.

"Someone has to play the part," he said bravely. "If I am to make acting my profession, I must be open to diversity." No one seemed to mind that Tom had appeared a little overconfident in his manner.

Mrs Trench looked at Tom in admiration.

Naomi Jones was given the role of Mary Magdalene, but didn't like it. She pulled a face.

"What's the matter, Naomi? Don't you want to be Carl's girlfriend?" teased Luke.

"Please, Miss, can I change? Can I play someone

else?" she begged, looking as if she was about to burst into tears. "I've heard the story about Mary Magdalene from my mum. She was, well -"

Naomi didn't get to finish explaining her reasons for rejecting the character she was asked to play, when Mary Stuart stepped forward.

"I'll do it Miss," she offered eagerly. "I'll take the role of Mary Magdalene." She smiled and looked up at Carl.

The teacher thought for a moment before she agreed to the change. So instead, Naomi accepted the part of Martha, one of Jesus' close friends. Pariah Gill, Naomi's Indian friend, looking humbled, accepted the role as Jesus' mother, Mary.

Many other roles were filled, including the rest of Jesus' disciples and a crowd scene. Finally, many songs were chosen, especially those written by the students and their music teacher, Miss Samantha Bloomington.

Mrs Trench told them of the final scene.

"In the final scene, you Carl McKenzie, as Jesus, dressed in typical Jewish clothes, will be seen in the garden agonising softly in song."

"*Oh no,*" squirmed Carl, disapprovingly. "I have to

sing as well?" He moaned and touched the sides his head, as if he was experiencing a sudden attack of intense pain.

Mrs Trench looked at Carl and shook her head before she continued. "Everyone, please be quiet and listen," she ordered, raising her voice above the din that had begun. "Jesus' disciples are asleep, but awoken as the Roman soldiers arrive, accompanied by Judas." Hush now prevailed in the room. The teacher looked over at Luke, adding, "Judas kisses Jesus -"

"Luke Reid, you have to kiss Carl, on the lips," interrupted Trevor Cartwright.

"No, I don't!" cried Luke, defiantly. He looked at the teacher for support.

"A quick peck on the cheek Luke, that is all," the teacher told him, herself looking amused. Then, turning to Trevor, she said, "Please stop teasing Trevor, or you may have to play Judas."

Carl looked wretched.

"As I was saying," continued Mrs Trench, "Jesus is arrested by the soldiers."

"After the kiss," muttered Trevor, with a smirk.

The teacher gave Trevor a disapproving glance as she continued.

"There will be a trial and Jesus will be condemned to death by the majority, those who call out the loudest for Barabbas to be freed - For those of you who might not be familiar with this particular biblical story, I will explain. Apparently, Barabbas was a very cruel man. Apart from his thieving ways, he had committed many atrocities, including murder and sedition."

Trevor nudged Craig, and whispered, "What's sedition?"

"That's when someone encourages people to go against the government and start trouble, like rioting and so on." Craig finished with a smug look on his face.

The teacher had pretended not to hear. "And he was the ring leader of many rebels," she said. "Incidentally, I have just realised, we haven't yet picked Barabbas, and we need someone to act this part. Who would like to be Barabbas in this play?" She looked around at glum-looking faces until her eyes rested on Carl, expectantly. She waited to hear whether he would ask to change roles, but he pouted, turned away and pretended to look through the window.

"I will Miss," cried Stanley. "Seeing it's only a pretend thing," he added, looking unembarrassed. Oddly enough, no one poked jokes or made any sly insensitive comments, at Stanley's choice of character.

Looking satisfied, Mrs Trench nodded and then began again. "We'll have a mournful song, while Jesus is seen bearing the heavy burden of the cross. We have a newcomer to our school, Trevor's twin sister, Gaia Cartwright. Welcome Gaia, I must admit, it is a most unusual arrangement, to have a new pupil join the school so late, and it is your last year at primary school. However, I have read the reason for your admittance. Do you think you will cope, leaving an all-girls' school to join a mixed school?"

"I think so Miss. I wasn't coping too well in an all-girls school. I know I'll only be here for two terms, but-but, I don't want to be home educated. I like being at school," explained Gaia, in a timid little voice.

"Yes, I understand Gaia," said Mrs Trench, "I think you are very brave."

"Thanks Miss," said Gaia.

"I would like you, Gaia," said the teacher with a friendly smile, "and the Buckling sisters, Kara and Sara, to sing this particular song." The teacher's announcement sounded so final that as a result no one complained.

"The song finishes and Jesus falls to the ground. Adam, you, playing Simon, will run over to Jesus, and you will relieve him of the cross." A broad grin transformed Adam's face, and exposed teeth that contrasted well with the colour of his skin, as the teacher continued, "A young woman will hurry over to Jesus, and will put a small mug of water towards his mouth. This is knocked from her hand and she is pushed aside by one of the Roman soldiers. Who will be that young woman and that particular soldier?" she asked. Not waiting for volunteers, Mrs Trench announced, "Gaia, you will be that young woman."

"Yes, Mrs Trench," replied Gaia, looking pleased. The teacher smiled and Gaia smiled back. Then she pointed to a young boy who had been chosen as one of the Roman soldiers. "You, Miles Carmender…."

Most of the children giggled.

"Oh boy," remarked Stanley. "I have heard some names, but yours, you've got to be kidding me." Stanley grinned and shook his head.

"His dad must be a mechanic," suggested Trevor.

Stanley stared blankly at Trevor.

"That's enough stirring from you two," the teacher advised, with a stern look. "You, Miles, will be that particular soldier."

"Thanks Miss. That's very kind of you," said Miles, looking and sounding surprisingly grateful.

Most of the youngsters giggled again, at Miles' modesty.

"You are most welcome, Miles," said Mrs Trench, before recommencing her explanation of the scene.

"A crowd will watch as the soldiers lead Jesus away. That's you Carl," the teacher reiterated pleasantly. Carl turned his gaze towards the floor, and the teacher ignored him, saying, "With Simon, that's you Adam, still bearing the burden of the cross and walking beside Jesus. All the cast will then look towards Jesus and Simon, while Craig leads them into a mournful song."

Craig received this bit of information looking quite elated.

"Jesus' disciples, fearful for their lives, gather in this large room. A short while afterwards, Jesus, dressed in white, enters, with two angels walking either side of him." The teacher turned to Mary. "You, Mary Stuart, who plays the part of Mary Magdalene, will announce loudly, looking joyous, but not over the top, Mary," she warned, "The Messiah, my Lord. He has risen! He's not dead he's alive!'"

13

Mary smiled and looked at Carl, but Carl, looking bashful, turned away.

Mrs Trench, looking pleased, smiled again before she continued, "Watching Jesus and the two angels walk off the stage and disappearing out of sight, you'll all begin to sing together, something cheerful, before the curtain falls."

"Can I be one of the angels, please Miss?" Patricia Moline eagerly offered with her hand up.

"Me too Miss," begged Trumpet Knowles, in a shy little voice. "Can I be one? I would like to be the other angel, Miss, please," he begged in a gentle voice.

Turning to face Patricia, Stanley, barked, "Girls can't be angels, fool."

"There are no fools in this room," Mrs Trench scolded, with a frown.

"Yes there is Miss," retorted Nikhil. "Stanley Baker, he is the fool because, I believe that there are male and female angels. There must be," he added, looking uncertain.

"Nikhil is right, angels can be male or female," suggested Carl, "and I know because em…." Suddenly conscious that all eyes were fixed on him, Carl fell silent.

"That does not justify calling anyone a fool," the teacher corrected.

"I guess not," Nikhil replied apologetically. Mrs Trench then turned to Carl.

"What were you about to explain about angels, Carl?"

"Oh, nothing, nothing Miss," replied Carl, sounding a little nervous.

"He's met an angel," teased Luke, and then he grinned playfully.

"No, he was once an angel, in heaven," remarked Stanley.

"Ha-ha, you two are so not funny," said Nikhil, in a sarcastic manner.

Many of the children giggled, but fell silent as their teacher looked over at Patricia, who had withdrawn from the front and was standing in a corner towards the back, sulking.

"There's no need to look so dejected, Pat," Carl encouraged.

Trevor mumbled, "Flip, here we go again, another stupid word."

Craig shook his head, "There's nothing stupid about

the word dejected, Trevor. If you read more and learn to use a dictionary, you would most probably learn the meaning of many words. To look dejected, is to look unhappy."

"Thank you for volunteering Patricia," said the teacher. "Of course you may. I think you will make an elegant-looking angel."

"Thanks Miss," said Patricia, becoming excited again.

Craig grinned mockingly, but Trevor, disagreeing, grumbled, "Whoever heard of a girl as an angel."

The teacher relaxed in her chair, and most of the children clapped excitedly and began to whisper to each other.

Carl didn't smile. He left the hall as soon as the end of school bell sounded. He did not wait for his friends, as he would normally do. He hurried to the bicycle shed, unchained his bike, jumped on it and rode off.

Chapter Two

The Offer

Carl was still fretting and complaining aloud to himself on his way home that afternoon.

"*Jeez*. Whatever next? Me, to dress as Jesus, and singing nonsense. I can't sing. I just wish I could get out of it," when Nikhil and Tom rode up beside him.

"Sorry, Carl," said Nikhil, sounding sympathetic, "but the part really suits you, and you might enjoy acting as Jesus."

Carl looked at his friend, lost his balance and the bicycle swerved, but he quickly got it back under control.

"I agree," said Tom, encouragingly. "It's not that it's for real, Carl. It's only a play. You said so yourself," he reminded, with a friendly smile.

"Yeah, I know, but–but, have you heard me sing? It's a bit extreme, don't you think? Can you see me all dressed up, *as Jesus*?" Carl examined himself.

Nikhil and Tom grinned at him. Then Tom said, "I have heard you sing, Carl. Aren't you forgetting? You sing all the time in church." He looked straight at Carl, and in all earnest he added, "I'll let you into a secret. Whenever I hear you sing, I always wish I could sing as good as you do."

"Yeah, right," said Carl, downheartedly.

"Come on, Carl," Tom coaxed. "Please cheer up, it's just for fun. Be honest, you playing the part of Jesus, it's not so bad, is it?"

"I guess not," replied Carl, in a quiet, subdued voice. But then Trevor, Luke and Craig, rode past them.

Luke yelled, "Jesus!"

Craig cried, "God man!"

And Trevor joined in, "Son of the Most High!"

Then the three boys laughed boisterously before Craig stressed in further amusement, "Is he a god?"

As the boys rode past, they pointed at Carl. Not paying attention, they collided and all three fell off their bicycles.

"Who has the last laugh now?" Carl shouted, as he, Tom and Nikhil, rode past them. They were sprawled out on the ground, with their bicycles beside them.

"Serves them right," said Nikhil, and he, Carl and Tom, laughed happily together.

Craig, Trevor and Luke, had scarcely gotten back up

onto their feet with their bicycles, when a man approached them from behind. They had not seen where he came from, but they turned to face him as he spoke.

This man looked like any ordinary person dressed in casual clothes.

"Hello, boys," he greeted. "I watched you fall off your cycles. None of you are hurt, I hope?" he enquired, looking intently at Craig.

"No I'm OK thanks," said Craig, in a suspicious manner.

"We are OK aren't we?" added Luke, nudging Trevor.

"Yeah, am OK, I'm not hurt," replied Trevor. He too looked distrustful at the stranger.

"Thank you for asking, that's very kind of you," Craig added and pushed forwards with his bicycle.

Trevor joined in again, "Yeah, thanks for showing concern, but there's no need."

They had not remounted, but had begun to walk on with their bicycles.

The stranger called after them, "Just a minute, boys."

They stopped and turned to face the man again.

"I don't mean to be rude, Sir," said Luke, "but what is it you want with us?"

"Yes, what do you want, Mister?" asked Craig. He sounded a little unpleasant. Luke and Trevor glanced sideways at their friend.

"You have an occasion coming up at your school, do you not?" the man enquired.

Clearly puzzled, the boys looked at each other, as if wondering how the stranger knew about their play. Perhaps he is one of the parents - Craig wondered to himself, before replying, "Yes, as a matter of fact, we do. But if you don't mind me asking, how do you know that? Who told you about our school musical?" Craig looked as if he was about to interrogate the man.

"Sensible questions," the stranger replied, and for the first time, a smile came over his face, which made him look quite pleasant. The boys looked at each other again, and it was evident that Trevor was beginning to become even more wary. Luke grinned nervously.

"Well, suppose I told you," the man continued, "there's very little I don't know about any of you." He had gestured quickly with his forefingers as he spoke.

"That's impossible! Please, do not insult my

intelligence," Craig retorted with a frown.

Trevor agreed, "Yes, that's impossible."

"Come on, let's go, he's clearly a wacko," suggested Luke, adding, "We don't know you and even if we did, how could you know everything about us?"

"Well, suppose I was to say...."

"You are not God," interrupted Craig, becoming defensive. "Only our parents, apart from God, would know everything about us. In fact, I believe that God knows more about us than our parents, I would say."

"Yeah, that's right," Trevor agreed boldly. "What is it you want with us, stranger?" he asked, an impertinent look on his face, as he began to scrutinise the man more thoroughly. "We shouldn't even be talking to you," he added.

"You are so right, and a sensible young boy," said the man. Then he smiled broadly, and once again, he looked intently at Craig, as he continued, "Suppose I told *you*, since you are the one who wishes to sing well at this special event...."

The boys gasped.

The man grinned. "As I said before, I know everything there is to know about the three of you and, as

I was about to let you know, I can cause it to be so that you, Craig...."

The friends looked flabbergasted.

The man looked amused. "Yes, you can have the most impeccable singing voice in the whole school. In fact..." he paused to laugh a little, "I can cause you young boy to sing better than any other person of your age, and it won't be just for this one occasion. This great singing voice would stay with you for many years to come. Just think about it," he encouraged, "you, young Craig...."

Craig, surprised to hear that this stranger from nowhere referred to him by his name, took a quick sharp breath, while Trevor and Luke, looked at each other, obviously as surprised as their friend.

The man looked elated. "You can become a great singer, amongst other things, whatever takes your fancy," he coaxed.

"Please, don't waste any more time trying to persuade us. I really don't know who you are, and as much as you appear to know my friend's name -"

"I know yours too, Trevor," interrupted the man.

Trevor nearly choked, but fought to disguise the fact that he was becoming more and more alarmed. He stared into the man's face.

"Even so, I must say, you sound as my friend just said." Trevor stuttered a little, and then he said, "*Crazy*, a real screw-ball, goodbye." Then, turning towards his friends, he asked, "Coming?"

"I'm coming," replied Luke.

The two boys remounted their bicycles.

"Bye for now, Luke," said the man, looking smug.

The fact that the man came out with his name, should not really have surprised Luke, but it did, he swayed to one side on his bicycle, but quickly rebalanced himself and rode on with Trevor. Craig stood looking at this unfamiliar person, as if he was in a daze and could not move.

"Craig, are you coming?" called Luke, in a loud voice, as he and Trevor began to ride away.

Craig gave no reply.

"Suit yourself," said Luke, and he and Trevor rode away, leaving their friend with a stranger. Craig, as if hypnotised by this man, did not notice when a small brown bottle suddenly appeared in the man's hand.

"Take this vial boy," said the man, slipping the tiny bottle into Craig's hand.

As if awakened from a dream, Craig looked from the man to the bottle in his hand. "Where are my friends and what's this for?" he asked.

"Your friends rode on. You'd better hurry along if you want to catch up with them, and think about wanting to sing your best, then drink from the vial and see what happens," the man told him.

Craig looked scornfully at the small bottle and then back at the man.

"I'm not supposed to accept gifts from strangers."

"Oh, but you can and you will," said the man.

"I can," said Craig. "But how do I know it's not poison, and that it will work?"

The man's light laughter brought Craig out of his enchanted state, "I bet it's a load of baloney," he said.

"You, young boy, like to ask double questions," the man replied. "If you believe the contents in the vial to be poison, throw it away. If not, *you must drink from it Craig. You have nothing to lose, but much to gain,"* and this time his look was piercingly hypnotic.

Craig pushed the small bottle into his pocket before looking at the man again.

"What have I got to lose? I could lose my life,

trusting a stranger." Craig sounded a little nervous.

The man's voice softened, "You won't. If you knew what I know about you, Craig, you would know I would never hurt you." Craig, looking confused, frowned. "Anyway," the man continued, "I promise you no harm will come to you, not from me. But you must promise me one thing in return," he coaxed.

"Yeah, and what's that?" asked Craig, as if regaining his composure.

"Your continued loyalty," he replied. "If you drink the contents of that vial, you won't die, and you will get what you desire, *but you will be one of my aides, when the time comes.* Just think how great it will be, after the first sip from that vial, you won't need to drink from it ever again. Just throw it in the river; your great singing voice will be automatic from then on."

Craig frowned.

"That sounds like quite an implausible suggestion," he said.

The man laughed.

"You have quite a way with words for a young boy, I'm impressed. Why don't you sleep on it, and if you should change your mind, don't drink from it, just smash the vial."

Craig took the bottle from his pocket and looked at it again.

"Here! What kind of prank is this?" he asked loudly. "It's empty. There's nothing in it!"

The man had disappeared and only his voice could be heard. "It won't be. As soon as you put it to your lips, it will be full to the brim, with flavour... Ha-Ha-aaa."

Craig, looking astonished, could hear the man's loud laughter, which continued for some time, as if it would never stop. He made to throw the bottle away, which under normal circumstances he would not have accepted, but he could not refuse the man's offer, and he could not throw the bottle away because, he was still under the man's hypnotic suggestion. He pushed it into his pocket again and looked around before he jumped on his bicycle and rode off.

Under this man's power of persuasion, Craig could not help himself, he had not discarded the bottle. He had kept it secretly hidden under his mattress. He knew what his parents would have said and done, and he didn't want to get in trouble, for breaking a most important rule, never to accept gifts from strangers. How would his parents have known or even believed that he had no choice in the matter? He said nothing to them, and had even kept it from his best friends.

On the morning before the concert began, all he could hear was the man's voice in his head, encouraging him to drink from the bottle. He had taken the bottle with him, so he slipped away, jumped on his bicycle and rode off to the river. Nervously, he did exactly as he was commanded and returned looking as he was feeling, a little nervous.

The school musical went down a treat, everyone who had an invitation attended, and even brought more family and friends along than were anticipated, so that the caretaker and some of the older boys in the school, had to go and get extra chairs from the storeroom. During the performance, Craig had a worried frown to begin with, until he took part in the first song, his frown, doubts and fears left him and he amazed everyone that day, including himself, with his splendid singing.

Ever-so-often, Craig tested his voice. His head swelled, and his pride grew bigger and bigger, from all the media attention and the many deals he was being offered by recording companies, to make him famous. His parents received several letters, even one asking their permission for him to take part in a famous singing show on television, but they turned down the invite.

Craig had no idea who he had met that day, nor what he would be called upon to do, in exchange for accepting the gift of his spectacular singing voice.

Chapter Three

Homes for Tom's Kittens

Two weeks after the Christmas holiday came and went, Tom was lying on the carpeted floor in their living room, making a great fuss of his pet cat Hildegard, who they all call Lady H, and her kittens, the four that were left that is. Two of the kittens had already been given away, but the black-and-white male he named Zack, they had decided to keep. The miracle kitten, Clovis, he hoped would become Gula and Carl's pet, and the ones promised to Mary and Craig, were yet to be homed.

He turned onto his side with his elbow on the floor, and rested his chin on the palm of his hand. He was feeling glad that all the anxieties over Clovis, were over, since Carl's sister, Gula, had given him healing a month before because, the tiny little kitten's life had instantly improved. Clovis was over two months old now, but there was still uncertainty as to whether Eleanor, Carl and Gula's mother, would allow the kitten in their home.

Tom recalled the weeks when he gave the first two kittens

away, to two of the children in year five at their school. How, before leaving, he had given Samantha Prince and Paul Headley, each of the kittens' new owner, a booklet, which he created entitled, Cats Health Advice and Guidance, by Tom Harper. He smiled pleasantly because he was feeling proud of his creation.

This little booklet gave practical advice on how to care for kittens and the suggested due dates for their injections, and other information such as having the kittens neutered. This was extremely important to Tom, so it was highlighted because he felt that awareness might help to prevent unwanted kittens being born. Lastly, it contained the contact number and address of their local vet, and a little map showing the directions to the surgery. He had also added his mother's mobile phone number, as he didn't have a mobile of his own. He wondered now whether adding his mother's number was a sensible thing to have done.

He looked solemnly at the mother cat, and then at Zack, lying by himself away from his three siblings. Two were stretched out with their front paws resting on their mother's body, and Clovis, had already walked over to him, and was lying close by. Tom stroked the kitten gently, and his mind drifted back to the last things he had said, after he had pointed out his mother's mobile phone number.

"Just in case, but only as a last resort, and you all know where I live so I haven't included my address, and please, don't ring my mother unnecessarily. Please bear in mind that unlike us, she has work to do." They had grinned happily at him.

A broad smile heightened his cheeks, remembering he had returned their cheeky grins. But his smile quickly melted away when he heard the doorbell rang. It was his friend, Mary, and her parents, Noel and Siobhan Stuart. It wasn't just Tom who looked surprised to see them, his parents, Pollyanna and Leslie, and his sister, Lucy, did too because the weather was so bad, it had snowed all day and hadn't let up. But an even greater surprise was the announcement Mary made as she walked towards the kitten of her choice.

"Tom," she said for everyone to hear, "I have chosen the name for my kitten. Sweetie, I'm calling her Sweetie."

The broad smile on Mary's face after her announcement quickly disappeared when Lucy cried, "Sweetie, what kind of a name is that?"

Mary's face went pale, "Well...she...she looks so sweet, that's why." Everyone laughed a little.

"Mary, how about Grey?" suggested her dad.

Mary's mother, had laughed at the name her husband suggested, and so did Mary, adding, "Don't be silly, dad."

Tom's parents had stood quietly observing, but the expression on Tom's sister's face, had enforced her disapproval, and Mary noticed.

"Tom," she said, looking a little self-conscious, "Do you like the name I have chosen for my kitten?"

Tom mused a little before he replied. "Sweetie, Sweetie, Mm. Well Mary, if that is how you feel about your kitten, I guess that's a good name. As long as *you* are happy calling the kitten, Sweetie, it is not for me or anyone else to say otherwise." He gave his sister a stern look.

"Thanks, Tom," said Mary, more cheerfully, and then she stooped down, picked up the kitten and began to stroke her gently. The kitten purred contentedly in her arms.

"She likes you already, Mary," said Pollyanna.

This pleased Mary so much, she laughed a little.

The little kitten meowed all the way to Mary's

32

home, and she continued fretting on and off for what seemed like ages afterwards. Tom had given Mary one of many familiar toys and a blanket to take home with her, as the blanket carried the kittens' and their mother's familiar smell, but Sweetie rejected them.

Before the kitten finally settled, she had toured the downstairs of the house, meowing in and out of every room. Finally, she hid herself away behind the large sofa in the living room, where she remained for some time. When at last she did emerge from her hiding place, she carried on fretting and sniffing around, until she eventually found what appeared to be a little comfort, on a cushion, in a corner near the radiator.

Mary had sat watching, and had endured little Sweetie's cries, hoping that she would stop, but the kitten was no doubt mourning the separation from her beloved mother, Lady H. This behaviour continued until her cries became occasional, and at times she would lift her little head and look over at Mary, who by this time was looking quite sorrowful.

It was not until near bedtime that Sweetie finally left her corner and hurried over to the two bowls Mary had prepared earlier. She ravenously ate some of the food and then drank a little water. For fear that the kitten might panic and start crying again, a delighted and relieved Mary, called out in almost a whisper to her parents.

"Dad, mum, she is eating. Sweetie is eating," she repeated happily.

"That's good," replied Siobhan, in an equally soft, but pleasing manner.

"It sure is," added Noel, warmly.

Mary turned to her father. "Does this mean she will settle now dad?" she asked.

Noel ignored Mary's question. "Perhaps now you can stop being so worried and eat a little supper before you go up to bed. You didn't touch any of the meal your mother took time to prepare."

At supper time, poor Mary had been full of anxiety over her new pet, which no amount of booklet reading could have prepared her for, and she had read a lot on the subject of how to take care of kittens. She would not have been able to eat a morsel, and she was looking downhearted. Siobhan and Noel, noticing, encouraged.

"Don't worry Mary, darling. Why don't you take Sweetie up to your room when you go up?" Noel suggested.

"Yes, that's a good idea Mary," agreed Siobhan. "Sit with her on your lap, if she will let you. Stroke her gently and say loving things to her."

Mary, feeling nervous, looked up at her mother.

"Like how happy you, we are that Sweetie has come to live with us, and how much you wanted her," continued Siobhan.

Mary gave a faint smile.

"Yes, and don't worry if she hides herself away for a while," put in Noel. "She'll soon come to you, poppet. She will soon feel at home here. Cats are easily adaptable creatures."

Noel smiled at Mary, but Mary still looked sad, so he gave her a lingering hug and a kiss on her cheek.

"She'll be settled by morning, you'll see," Siobhan further encouraged, after she had kissed Mary's forehead.

"Can she sleep on my bed tonight mum?" asked Mary.

"Yes, I don't see the harm in that, but only if she wants to mind, and leave your room door open so that she will be free to leave if she wants to."

"Thanks mum," said Mary, sounding much brighter than before.

"Wait just a minute, has the kitten been trained?" asked Noel.

"Trained?" repeated Siobhan, giving her husband a curious look.

"You know, potty trained, I mean, to use the litter tray," replied Noel, wide-eyed. "I hope I am not expected to give a hand when the mess needs to be cleaned up around here," he joked.

"You don't have to help take care of the kitten, Mary and I will see to her, and perhaps you can see to yourself for a change," teased Siobhan.

Siobhan gave Mary another comforting hug, and then she walked out of the living room and headed upstairs to her own bedroom, with Noel following behind her muttering, "I must remember to buy an air freshener in the morning, first thing. I wonder if one will be enough," he added.

Siobhan looked at him, smiled, and shook her head.

Chapter Four

Indecisions

The week when it was Craig's turn to collect his pet kitten, he and his parents, Stella and Brian, had borrowed a carrier to accommodate the kitten he had chosen, or rather, the kitten his mother had chosen.

Tom had felt that a gradual separation from her kittens would be kinder to Lady H, who appeared to be unusually fond of them, and so he had allowed a whole week to go by, before giving away each kitten.

Initially, Craig had chosen the kitten Tom had named Zack, and he wanted to name him Tigger, but when Stella looked at the kitten, for reasons she never mentioned, she didn't take a fancy to him.

"No darling, don't be so hasty. Let us look at the others first," she said, while looking a little scornful. Lucy, noticing, opened her mouth. She had the urge to ask Stella, not to turn her nose up at Zack, but had second thoughts. She took a deep breath instead and then exhaled heavily before she closed her mouth.

Pollyanna looked away from Stella, and briefly gazed at the very tall young boy, who sat wishing for the kitten of his choice - What chance has he of getting his mother to let him choose - She thought to herself.

"Chance would be a fine thing," suddenly slipped out of her mouth.

"What did you say honey?" asked Leslie, their eyes meeting briefly.

Pollyanna did not reply because she was still preoccupied, thinking how tall Craig had grown, which didn't surprise her because, Stella was six feet tall, and Brian was even taller.

After what seemed like a rather long deliberation between Craig, and his mother and father, his mother finally chose the tabby, but her choice was short lived as Tom stepped in quickly.

"I am sorry, Stella, but that's Clovis, and he is already taken."

Tom had a determined look on his face, a look the rest of his family had never seen before. He picked up the kitten, stepped backwards, bumped into the coffee table and fell onto his back, with his legs up in the air and both hands holding Clovis, up in the air, in the middle of the living room. Everyone but Stella saw the funny side of it and laughed, but she stood with pouted lips, which made her face looked even longer than it really was. Tom, showing how agile he was, sprang back up onto his feet, his face flushed, stroking the kitten gently. Clovis stared at Stella and then at Tom. Any other kitten would have become startled, and would have more than likely wriggled out of his hands and scampered away, but not Clovis, he began to purr contentedly in Tom's arms.

Stella turned to face Tom, looking disappointed.

"Taken, taken by whom? Then why is he still here?" she protested.

"He is here, Stella, because Carl needs to buy a cat carrier to take him home in." Tom looked innocent. He knew that whenever Stella got an idea fixed in her mind, it could be hard to get her to change it. Most people always gave in to her, but Tom, he wasn't about to, not this time. He also figured that a little white lie, would not do any harm, since he wasn't about to break his promise to his best friend.

Pollyanna offered and took orders for tea and hot buttered scones, with jam, as an added extra. Afterwards, she excused herself and quickly exited to the kitchen, leaving her husband, her son and her daughter to deal with Stella.

Tom also remembered that he had been forewarned. He had made up his mind from that surprising day that he wouldn't let Lady H's last kitten go to any other family, not until he was absolutely certain that Carl's mother would not allow Carl and Gula, to have him. If that turned out to be the case, he had also decided that he would keep the kitten. This way he concluded, Carl and Gula would be able to see Clovis, as often as they liked.

"Oh, I see," Stella remarked, her voice softening, "Eleanor is allowing Carl and Gula, to have a kitten after all. That is good, I am glad. I am so pleased for Carl," she added, sounding more relaxed.

Lucy looked at Stella and mumbled to herself, "Right, you reckon. You are just about as pleased as I am. I don't want Clovis to leave my family, and you, Stella, you *do* mind that the kitten is promised to someone else, I am sure of it.'

Pollyanna returned to the living room. Stella had lightened up a little and her accent sounded even posher than Craig's. She sighed. "Well, let me see," she said, turning towards Lady H, and pretending to be jolly. At that moment, Lucy noticed that Craig had two fingers on each hand crossed behind his back. She guessed it was in the hope that his mother would change her mind and choose Zack after all. This did make Lucy smirk a little.

Sadly for Craig, it wasn't to be. Stella screwed up her face and wrinkled her nose whenever Zack walked past her or dared to brush against the long black velvet skirt she was wearing. It was as if a bad smell had suddenly entered the room or she had tasted something sour. Afraid that his mother might change her mind and not let him have his pet, Craig settled for the kitten of her choice.

Lucy sat quietly thinking Craig was rather a wimp, and frightened that she might let something slip, something, which once again she felt like saying aloud, but didn't dare, remembering the day she was allowed on her dad's boat on the river, with Craig and his father, and knowing that her naughty behaviour, had nearly caused the boat to capsize.

"If I misbehave at any time soon, dad will ground me for six months, for sure," she mumbled to herself again.

One by one, they helped themselves to tea and sat down.

"In that case, I shall choose," said Stella, ignoring the mug of tea her husband had stretched towards her. Brian cleared his throat and placed the mug back on the table.

Satisfied or not, Stella had chosen the kitten she felt was the next best, but Lucy really could not understand how she had reached that conclusion because, as far as she was concerned, all the kittens had their own little peculiarities about them, but they were all quite cute and special.

The kitten Stella picked was a plain, long-haired chocolate-coated one. Soft and fluffy to the touch, but she had big, round, staring eyes, and she gave intimidating stares, particularly when she saw anyone for the first time. Her stares would be long and hard, and a little terrifying to look at, which proved very disturbing at times, especially to children and those who disliked cats. Zack's peculiarity was that he would hiss, showing all his teeth, rather like a big massive grin, then he would give a snarl or two before walking away, after realising no one was really afraid of him.

"Yes, hurray!" Craig declared, jumping up from his seat. "I was hoping you would choose her, mum," he said, pretending to be excited, but Lucy could tell by the look on his face afterwards, that he wasn't really being up front about it.

"She looks like a little Cleo, indeed," said Brian.

"Oh no, don't be silly darling. Let us choose the other name that Craig thought of. She looks like a Tigger to me." No one was convinced because Stella was being so indecisive. She contemplated for a while. Finally she said, "I think we should let Craig decide. I think that would be the best thing. After all, the kitten is going to be his pet." Stella called out to Craig, as if he was partially deaf or not really in the room. "Craig, what do you think? Does dumplings here look like a Tigger or a Cleo to you?"

"Oh no!" cried Craig. "You are not going to call her Dumplings, are you mother?" Craig looked confused.

Everyone laughed at the idea.

"Don't be silly Craig," said Stella. "You are afraid that I will name the kitten, Dumpling. For goodness sake child, I just asked you what you thought of the names, Tigger or Cleo."

Craig immediately relaxed. "Oh yes, Cleo is a good name," he agreed hastily, pretending to be happy.

"Tigger it is then," put in Brian, with an impatient expression on his face.

Chapter Five

Warnings Ignored

The School was in a good location. It was set well back from the main road, with two large car parks across the road from the school buildings, one designated strictly for the teaching staff and the other for visitors. The large historic building was once a small palace, on several acres of land, with well-kept gardens and woodland.

The playing field and sports ground were situated mainly to the back of the building. There was a large school library in a separate building nearby, with an adjoining theatre, which had a good-sized stage, and a school shop. Apart from the ordinary play areas, the school also had its own indoor and outdoor swimming pool, a football pitch, a tennis court, and a hockey pitch.

Wooden benches were placed in designated areas, such as under a large oak tree in sight of a running stream and well-designed flower beds. There was also a water fountain, a large fish pond, and a rockery with especially low-growing colourful hardy plants; such as gentian and heathers, growing in between them. Not to forget the herb garden. There were also many different trees, some dating back hundreds of years. The woodland attracted many different kinds of wildlife all year round. Shrubs and different scented wild flowers were a delight in the spring and summer, and evergreens in the autumn and winter months prolonged the thought of summer.

On certain occasions, the children not only took nature walks with their teachers, but independently, due to their own liking of the place. It quickly became a special place to hang out all year round, as each season had its own beauty and interest. Carl, Tom and their friends liked to take their lunches there in the summer.

The land was so vast that there were set boundary rules, as to how far into the woods the children were permitted to go by themselves. But one day, ignoring the two large signs, 'Do not go beyond this point,' two children wondered off and became entangled. Unseen by them, giant vines slowly and timely unwound from two huge peculiar looking trees, and crawled along behind the children.

Preoccupied with other interests, they did not notice what was about to befall them, until they found themselves being bound like balls of wool by the vines.

They screamed, kicked and fought with their hands and feet, but their efforts were no match for the vines. The vines wrapped themselves around them until only their eyes were noticeable.

It took many staff, children and other outside volunteers, to search for them in the woodland, and by the time they were finally discovered, the two pupils were barely alive, and the vines had grown stouter in size. It was obvious to all who had joined in the search, that there was no way the children could be set free from their entrapment. Every effort to free them from the leaches, as the vines were nicknamed, was proving tedious and impossible.

One of the children was Carl's cousin, Nicholas Ogilvy. Tom noticed that his friend had become emotional. Carl was tearful as they stood helplessly watching and secretly wishing for a way to save them. His hands were wet from wiping away his tears, when he saw his cousin's eyes closed. He ran towards Nicholas through the sorrowful, helpless looking crowd, and a man called to him to stop, but he ignored him.

Tom followed Carl to the spot where the two children were bound to the trees by the stout vines. He watched as Carl touched his cousin's eyes, with hands wet from tears. He had touched the big twisty vines on both trees in the process. To the utter delight and amazement of everyone that day, the vines began to unwind themselves from around the children, and eventually withered and died, even the peculiar looking trees withered away.

The children were barely alive because the vines had nearly sucked the life out of them. But thankfully, after a simple unexplainable act performed by Carl, they were both freed, and after an examination by a doctor, it was announced that they would survive. The other amazing thing was, they did not need blood transfusions to replace the blood that had been sucked from them by the blood sucking vines. Relieved, but clearly puzzled, no one understood what had taken place that day.

In assembly the following morning, the head teacher, Mr Railways, spoke about what had happened, saying, he believed it could only have been a miracle from God, who watches over his creation. He further warned of long periods of detention, for any pupil who goes into the woods without permission, and for those who venture beyond the set boundaries unaccompanied or unsupervised by a member of staff.

On this particular Thursday, the day was dry and sunny, but quite chilly, even when the sun shone through. Miss Jacinta Mulish, the history and geography teacher, stood looking out through the window of her classroom, room G6. As her class arrived, she waited until all the pupils were settled in their chosen seats before she turned to face them.

"Good morning, G6!" she greeted cheerfully.

"Good morning, Miss Mulish!" chorused the children in the same tone of voice, as if to imitate their class teacher.

The teacher smiled then turned to face the window again.

"What a pleasant day!" she announced.

The youngsters did not respond.

In a dream-like manner she began.

"'How do I love thee? Let me count the ways.'"

Unnoticed by Miss Mulish, the children looked at each other, clearly surprised and puzzled, as their teacher continued.

"'I love thee to the depth and breadth and
    height my soul can reach...' " she recited.

Miss Mulish was not much taller than Mary Stuart,

but the height of her heels made her look taller than her five feet one inch. She swung round dramatically to face the children again, and in a high-pitched tone of voice, she continued.

"'When reaching out of sight, for

the ends of being an ideal grace.

I love thee to the level of every day's

most quiet need, by sun and candlelight.'"

She had gestured with both hands as she spoke the last two lines.

A fit of giggles erupted in the classroom, and a few of the boys and girls even pretended to clap their hands in amusement, until Luke Reid raised his hand.

"Thank you, little ones," said Miss Mulish, with a delighted look on her face. "What is it, Luke?" she asked, a kind of quaintness to her voice.

"Are we having a poetry lesson instead of geography today, Miss? And isn't that a rather old love poem you are reciting Miss Mulish?" he asked, all in one breath.

"Yes, it is, it is a love poem. Do you know it, Luke?" she asked, enthusiastically.

"No, Miss," Luke replied in a dull kind of voice. "I

hope you don't mind me saying, Miss, but you... I mean... it sounds silly, the *poem* that is. I don't like love poems. I know it because I became tired of hearing my mother practising it for her elocution classes, when I was younger. I had wished never to hear it again." Luke pulled a face. The rest of the class giggled playfully again.

"If you must know, I am reciting this short poem, as a tribute to this day."

Some of the children spluttered.

"Tribute, Miss?" asked Patricia Moline, looking amused. Sean Sculley's whole body shook. He was having an uncontrollable fit of the giggles.

"My mum loves that poem," said Patricia.

The others looked quite surprised, for Patricia was one of the children who very rarely spoke out so bravely in class, unless she was asked to do so. They turned towards her.

"Does she, Patricia?" their teacher asked. "In that case, your mother and I must have something in common," she suggested, with a delighted look on her small oval-shaped face.

"No, not at all, Miss," Craig offered. "You and Carmen, Mrs Moline, that is Patricia's mum, have nothing whatsoever in common. In fact, you couldn't be more different."

Miss Mulish ignored the mischievous laughter, which could be heard coming mostly from the back of the classroom.

"We share the same taste in something," she prompted, not at all irritated by Craig's remark.

Sarcastically, Craig replied, "Yes, *one poem*."

"If I may be allowed to finish what I was saying before I was so rudely interrupted," announced Patricia, with an endearing look on her face.

"Go ahead my dear," Miss Mulish encouraged eagerly.

"Mum normally says it, the poem, to all her boyfriends, when she's dressed up ready to go out and they call for her. Not all at once. She has about three, maybe four. Mum told me that it was written by a woman named Elizabeth Barrett-Browning. I am sick of hearing it."

"Are we or are we not having a geography lesson today, Miss?" interrupted Nikhil, looking bored.

"Yes, of course we are," responded Miss Mulish, whose name really suited her.

"Let's get on with it then," said Stanley Baker under his breath.

The children became boisterous, until their teacher's voice rose above theirs, and brought about silence.

"Pupils, I have developed the habit of reciting this particular poem, whenever the day is a pleasant one, and today is indeed a pleasant-looking day, don't you all agree? The sky is blue, the sun is shining," she added in forced pleasantry.

"So it is, Miss Mulish," joined Craig, in pretend dreamlike manner, which surprised the rest of the class, including the teacher herself.

"I am truly thankful that the cold weather has abated. I simply detest the cold weather," she admitted.

"*Abated,* Miss?" asked Omotayo Igbo.

"Yes, Omotayo, abated, it has become less cold," the teacher replied brightly.

"Thank you Miss," said Omotayo, politely. "My dad uses words like that one."

The teacher sighed. "It has been a hard winter. We should all feel happier today. Let us hope this good weather continues," she added.

"I don't. I do not feel happy," grumbled Naomi Jones, who looked thoroughly miserable. "Why must I when my mother went off to Japan and left me with my grumpy dad and not my grandparents, even though I begged to be allowed to stay with them?" Naomi's Japanese accent, which was only sometimes apparent, was obvious. Carl turned his head towards the short, slim, mixed-race girl seated four desks away from him. A faint smile had outlined the corners of his mouth, and for a moment or two, he became fascinated by her - This is remarkable - he thought - for a ten-year-old girl who has spent almost all of her life, so far, in England.

"Naomi, I am sure your father is not a grumpy man," Miss Mulish replied, "You are just a hard-to-please child."

Naomi muttered something, which sounded inaudible to the teacher, but caused the rest of the class to giggle rather loudly this time.

"Giggles!" cried Miss Mulish, who had raised her voice above the loud outburst. "Won't someone share the joke with me?" The teacher waited, but no one responded to her request.

Miss Mulish looked towards the large double

windows again. She sniffed a little.

"Spring is in the air. Can you not smell it pupils?" she asked, and then she sniffed again. What sounded like the whole class then copied her.

"No, Miss," almost all of them chorused.

"Well, *I* say it is and *I* smell it," continued the teacher. "Listen everyone," she paused and tilted her head to one side and listened, then said, "the birds are singing too."

Laughter immediately exploded in the classroom.

Stanley Baker, who was sitting in his usual seat at the back, which no one else dared occupy, shouted to the teacher.

"Singing, Miss. I didn't know birds sing."

"Well, Mr Baker, now you know," she replied.

The boy seated next to Stanley, turned and poked his tongue out at him, only to be jabbed with a pencil on the back of his hand.

"Ouch!" cried the boy.

"Stop laughing, all of you," ordered Miss Mulish. "And you, Stanley Baker, I saw that." She pointed. "You will not only apologise to Trumpet this minute, but you will stay behind after the lesson."

Carl looked over in the boy's direction. He wondered why he was named Trumpet, because he was as quiet as a mouse.

Stanley muttered a quick, insincere, "Sorry," then, "Dog's breath," which only Trumpet and those sitting close by heard.

"Birds don't sing, Miss," Craig announced boldly.

This brought about silence once more.

"Don't they?" asked their teacher.

"No, they chirp, Miss," Craig informed her.

The teacher paced up and down nearly the whole length of the classroom before she walked back over to the window, and as she turned to face the children, the rays from the sun hit her already full head of white hair. It caused her hair to look silvery, and her brown face seemed to take on a peculiar radiance as the shaft of sunlight briefly passed over her.

"When birds are chirping, they are singing," she informed the class in a firm manner, but Craig persisted in his adamant and posh way of speaking.

"Birds cannot sing, they *chirp*, which incidentally is a short high-pitched sound. That information is for you, Miss Mulish, and of course, for the rest of the class. At least, for those who do not know the meaning of the term, 'to *chirp*.'" He had emphasised again, finishing with a slight nod of his head, showing satisfaction.

"Obstinate teenager!" cried the teacher. "For your persistence, you will write fifty times, 'When birds are chirping, they are really singing'."

"I will not. And I am not a teenager. I will not become twelve for another month. A teenager begins at thirteen," retorted Craig.

"That is true, Miss," agreed Trevor.

"What is true?" snapped the teacher, giving Trevor an intense look. "Would you like to join him?" she asked, letting her Asian accent slip in.

"No, Miss," replied Trevor, "but–but–"

"But–but what?" asked the teacher firmly.

Surprisingly, Miss Mulish had suddenly taken on a totally different personality. Trevor fell silent.

The teacher looked from Craig to Trevor.

"In that case, you Trevor Cartwright, you will write the same statement as Craig, but *One hundred* times."

In disbelief, Gaia cried, "One hundred times!"

Miss Mulish looked triumphant.

"That is unfair," argued Gaia.

"Would you Gaia Cartwright, like to take your brother's place? Well, would you?" she snapped.

"No, Miss," replied Gaia, in a subdued manner.

"Trevor, it's either that or you and Craig, can volunteer to help the caretaker free the school playground of unwanted leaves," offered Miss Mulish.

The boys could not conceal the rigid expressions, which instantly transformed their faces.

Craig spoke softly at first. "I will not be assisting anyone to clean up the school grounds, and Trevor can write lines. *Fool!*" he cried raising his voice, "I didn't ask him to stick up for me." Craig got into a fit of temper. "I certainly won't be writing any lines either because, you might be our geography teacher, but I know that I am right, you just can't or won't admit it. Besides, you have just wasted a quarter of our lesson time on gibberish talk. Being only a supply teacher, you may or may not know this, but my mother is on the board of governors. She will hear about this from me that I can assure you Miss Mulish."

Miss Mulish, in a forceful manner, replied.

"Craig Brackenridge, for your insolence you will extend the lines by adding, I must believe my teacher and will not be so confrontational and contradictory, and you will write the same amount of lines as Trevor, one hundred."

Craig stood up. He pushed his hands in his pockets.

"I will do no such thing!" he yelled defensively.

"And I must never yell in class," yelled the teacher. "You will add that, too. And take those hands out of your pockets immediately," she ordered. But it didn't stop Craig's bold protest, as he reluctantly pulled one hand then the other out of his pockets, watched by the teacher and the rest of the class.

"If you want to see that on paper, *you* write it. I will not. And if you want to help the caretaker with his cleaning, *you* go and do it," he remarked, sounding even more defiant.

"I agree," Trevor joined in, while the rest of the class looked on, intrigued and extremely stimulated.

"Craig and Trevor, you will both write the same lines, adding, 'I must not unduly waste time in class and I must not disrespect any of my teachers'."

"That's a laugh," responded Craig, sounding almost comical, "us wasting time, what an understatement."

Miss Mulish gave Craig a sharp look, and then she stared at Trevor, as if daring him to speak.

"I don't know what you mean, Miss," said Trevor, low-spiritedly.

"You don't know what I mean. What do you mean you don't know what I mean?"

"Unduly, Miss, am I being unduly?"

"Trevor, unduly means excessive," volunteered Craig, in heightened frustration.

Trevor looked even more confused.

"What has excessive got to do with me, Miss?" he asked.

"She means, you geek, are behaving in an improper, or unjustifiable manner," snapped Craig.

Trevor, looking even more perplexed, began to twiddle his thumbs.

"That is exactly what I mean you *both* are," was the teacher's bold response, adding, "Now, Craig, you will sit down, and both of you will write the lines while the rest of the class get on with copying and filling in the map that is on the board, in their exercise books."

Neither Craig nor Trevor did as they were told, and so they were both ordered to return to the class after school, for detention.

Stanley Baker had been detained for what he had done to Trumpet Knowles, earlier. He was seated in his usual seat at the back of the class when the two boys walked in. He looked at them and grinned mischievously.

"You two did well to turn up," Miss Mulish announced. "You, Craig, and Trevor," she said, looking stern, "get on with writing the lines while I go to the office to phone your parents. The two boys sat sulking while Miss Mulish dismissed her last class of the day. As soon as she left the room, Craig had a change of mind.

"You can allow yourself to be detained," he said, still grumpy, "but me, I will not. There was only one person wasting time in class, and that was Miss Mulish. She knows she is not allowed to detain us unless she gives our parents prior notice, that rule has not been changed. When I tell my parents what happened in her lesson, I promise you she won't be employed at this school for more than another week, if that."

"Yeah, let's go," agreed Trevor.

The two boys grinned at each other. Then, making sure the teacher was nowhere in sight, they left the classroom and hurried out of the school.

Chapter Six

A Barge Ride

Every effort was being made in the hope that Eleanor would have a change of heart pretty soon and allow Carl and Gula, to take Clovis home. It was no longer just Carl and his sister hoping, it had become a team effort.

As an added extra, Gula created what she called her own little rituals, which she did often and alone. She had begged her mother for a little round wooded table and one of her white embroidered table cloths. She placed the table at one corner of her bedroom and covered it with the cloth. Then she went to the bank and withdrew a whole month's money from her savings, and went shopping. From the village market stalls, she purchased a pink candle in a candle holder, a few crystals, a box of her favourite incense sticks and an incense burner.

It was almost lunch time when she returned home. She was feeling so elated that she could not wait until after she had lunch, to arrange the things she had bought unto her table. She begged her mother to allow her to eat a little later and immediately set to work. She placed a picture of Clovis and a picture of her mother on the table, together with the candle in its holder, the crystals, and one of the incense sticks, which she placed in an incense burner.

Gula then sat cross legged in front of the well-dressed table, looking pleased. She bowed then made the sign of the cross and began to recite the Hail Mary prayer, three times. Afterwards, she sat for ages with her eyes closed, silently meditating. She imagined the family bringing Clovis home to live with them.

This became a regular practice each day after school, even before she did her homework. When she wasn't praying to Mary, the mother of Jesus, she would call to specific angels, asking them to help her mother to get over her fear of cats. At times this annoyed her brother because, he would be out in the garden playing with his friends, and they would hear her, especially when she was chanting a Buddhist chant, *'nam-myoho-renge-kyo'*, repetitively, which she learnt from her Buddhist friend Noriko. She always left asking for help from the Egyptian cat goddess, Bastet, until last.

No one could enter while she was practicing her rituals, and when they were allowed to enter her room, no one was allowed to touch anything on her table.

Tom, Mary, and even Nikhil, had joined in sending up prayers on Carl's behalf. Although Gula claimed hers were different. She claimed she was not simply praying, but that she was also petitioning, which to her was more important than just saying ordinary everyday prayers.

From Lady H's pregnancy to the birth of her kittens, there had never been a dull moment in the Harper household. There had been happening after happening, and this particular day was no exception. No one understood how Zack had gotten up onto the roof of their house. Lucy was the first to spot him and alerted the rest of her family.

"Mum, dad, Tom!" she yelled at the top of her voice. "Come quickly. It's Zack, he's stuck. He is on the roof and I don't think he knows how to get back down!"

Pollyanna was the first to rush through the back doorway.

"Oh, goodness me!" she exclaimed. "How on earth did Zack get up there?"

"He got up using his four legs, mother," said Tom,

who had joined them, looking displeased. "There is no need for any of us to guess how Zack got out of the house. We all know that," he continued, his face turning red with anger.

"What are you suggesting, Tom?" asked Pollyanna.

"I am not suggesting anything, mother. I am simply stating the fact that only Lucy would have been dumb enough to have opened the door and let him out."

Lucy gasped as Tom continued. "Only Lucy would leave him out here to climb up onto the roof," he further accused.

"Oh, right, I see," said Pollyanna, turning to face Lucy, who stood blushing bright pink. "Lucy, what have you got to say for yourself?" she asked.

Lucy looked away. "How was I to know that he wouldn't follow me back inside? I only went outside for a minute, and came back in and..."

"And you didn't bother to pick him up and bring him back indoors!" yelled Tom. "You can go and fetch the ladder and you can climb up and get him," he ordered, his temper growing.

"Me, I can't do that!" cried Lucy, becoming even redder in the face.

"Well, *I* won't be climbing the ladder," said Tom.

Zack was sitting in the middle of the roof, meowing and looking around, when Leslie walked through the doorway carrying the ladder. He secured it against the wall of the house and began to climb. But as he neared the top, he stopped because Zack had gotten up, stretched and began to walk towards him. Leslie stretched out his hands and beckoned to the kitten.

"Good Zack, that's a good cat. Come to me, let me help you get down off this place," he encouraged. "Come kitty, kitty, kitty."

Zack stopped, looked at Leslie, then turned and walked to the far end of the roof, away from him, and sat down at the edge nearest to the drainpipe.

"Do you think he is going to jump or go down the pipe?" asked Lucy, pulling a face.

"If he does and he gets stuck or hurt, you know who is to blame," said Tom, giving his sister a displeasing look.

Leslie climbed to the top and sat at the edge beside the ladder, he had continued to try and coax the kitten to walk over to him, but Zack took no notice, he meowed even louder than before, looking around.

"He is frightened," said Tom.

"Yes, I agree," said Pollyanna. "Where is Lady H? Go and get her, Tom. Perhaps she will climb up and get Zack off the roof," she suggested.

"She is not inside either," said Lucy.

"What do you mean she is not inside? You let Lady H, out too? And I suppose Clovis is with her." said Pollyanna, in growing frustration.

Lucy screamed, "I couldn't stop them, they... they ran out after me!"

"Lucy, for heaven's sake, stop shouting," said Pollyanna, looking at her crossly. "Why didn't you alert one of us before now? I really don't blame Tom for being mad at you, you thoughtless child. You had better go and find Lady H, and Clovis, and bring them home my girl," she scolded.

Tom rested both hands on his head and turned away from his family, looking bewildered. "I cannot believe that out of all the sisters in this world, I had to end up with you," he complained, walking away. "I'll go and find my cat and her kitten."

Realising he was being followed, he turned to face his sister.

"Lucy, don't you follow me, go look over there," he snapped, pointing away from him. But then they noticed Lady H had appeared at the other end of the roof top and was meowing.

Zack got up and walked halfway towards his mother, but then he stopped and looked around once more before he recommenced his cries. He must have been calling to Lady H because she meowed back and Zack became silent, sat down and watched his mother walking towards him.

"Good cat, good Hildegard, that's real good Lady H, go get your kitten and take him off this roof that's a good lady," encouraged Leslie.

Lady H, picked the kitten up in her mouth, trotted past Leslie and stepped onto the top rung of the ladder. Leslie turned and his foot accidentally caught the ladder and pushed it forwards, sending it and the mother cat, with her kitten still in her mouth, into the air.

"Oh no!" cried Tom.

"Dear me!" yelled Pollyanna.

Lucy looked shocked. There was nothing any of them could have done at that moment because, they were taken by surprise. They stood and watched the ladder as it landed on the ground. Lady H and her kitten were flung over and down towards the river.

"My cat, Lady H, Zack, they'll drown!" yelled Tom, running to look over into the water. But luckily for them, Lady H with Zack still held firmly in her mouth, had landed on all fours in a passing barge.

"Thank God," whispered Tom. "She has not fallen into the river, she is on the barge and I think she is OK."

Lucy had not seen when the grey fog appeared and transformed itself into a giant man, who had stretched his great big hand down to the ground, had picked up Zack and placed him on top of the roof. He shape shifted back into the fog and evaporated into thin air. Not one of them had noticed Clovis because he had made himself invisible to them. He had stood on the other end of the roof, up on his hind legs, with his front paws motioning in the air. He had sent a golden ray that had formed beneath Lady H, protecting her and her kitten and then vanished as soon as they had landed safely in the barge.

The tall stout man on the barge, who had watched the cat and her kitten's descent and landing, shook his head, waved at Leslie and he waved back.

"That was a spot of luck," said Leslie, as he and

Pollyanna breathed a sigh of relief.

"That's Dennis Hopper, the new chap who has moved into Betty's old cottage. He inherited the cottage when Betty died, he's her grandson."

"I didn't know old Betty had a grandson. I didn't know she had any relatives," said Pollyanna, showing interest. To think, all those years she lived in that cottage alone, not once did he visit her. During my visits to her, she had never once mentioned him. The disappointed look left her face. "Anyway, thank goodness that barge was passing. If not, I don't know what would have happened to Lady H and Zack, there's no bank from here to the clearing."

"Dennis knows that Lady H and her kitten belong to us," said Leslie. "I am sure he will stop down by the clearing. I'll drive down and get them."

"Wait, please dad," said Tom. "I'm coming with you. I'll just get the carrier." Tom ran inside and in no time returned with a large cat basket.

"I'm coming too," said Lucy.

"Oh no, you are not," said Pollyanna, as she picked up the ladder and rested it against the side of the house. "You, Lucy, have work to do, inside."

"Work to do," repeated Lucy, reluctantly.

"Yes, *work* to do, and you can begin by emptying, washing and drying the cat bowls and filling them with fresh food and water. You can then change the litter trays, and after that, see to their baskets."

"Oh, that's so unfair!" cried Lucy.

"I am being unfair? In that case, when you have finished, you can vacuum the living room," ordered Pollyanna, walking back inside the house.

Lucy stomped her way in behind her mother, sulking.

Pollyanna turned to face her. "We have all been busy helping Zack and forgot about Clovis. Lucy, where is Clovis?" she asked, with an accusing look on her face.

Lucy went pale and stared at her mother, she was speechless.

"Don't tell me, Lucy!" yelled Pollyanna.

Clovis suddenly appeared from behind the settee, meowed and rubbed himself against Pollyanna's leg and then he looked up at her.

Calm down, he said, or you might just pop an artery! It's been an eventful day, I know, but everyone's fine. It wasn't all the kid's fault. Zack couldn't have gotten up there by himself – think about it. I saw who took him and put him on the roof, and I know why the fiend did it, but it's not my time yet, so I had to stand by and let it happen. I couldn't 'let the cat out of the bag,' so to speak. Clovis gave a throaty chuckle - *It's too soon. You, Pollyanna, for one, you aren't ready to realise me*, he said - *Really, there is no need to be so hard on the kid*.

Clovis looked up at Pollyanna and scratched the sides of his head. Pollyanna noticed.

"I must give those claws a cut," she said, bending over and stroking him then she smiled and walked away.

Clovis looked over at Lucy.

Your mother can't hear me, can she? I forgot, and neither can you - he added, walking away swishing his tail in the air.

Chapter Seven

The Inner Voice

Tom had noticed over the following weeks that on the odd occasion, Clovis would suddenly wink an eye. The first time it happened, he had assumed that the kitten had developed a nervous twitch, which would go away after a while. But as it didn't, not entirely, Tom decided that it was most peculiar, especially since the kitten would deliberately look at him and then wink, like a human being would. Another remarkable thing was, whenever Clovis winked at him, he could almost guarantee that something was about to happen, or had just happened.

On this particular Friday, in the early evening, Clovis winked at Tom, jumped onto his lap, yawned, stretched, and then rubbed his knees with his two front paws. He then stretched out across Tom's lap, and there he remained with his eyes closed. For a moment, Clovis actually looked as though he had fallen asleep, he had become so still, and Tom did not hear him purring, not even once. They remained in the same position for ages, as if the boy and the young cat were having their portrait painted.

On that same day, Pollyanna had a call from Leslie, after which she told the children that their Grandma Gertrude, had fallen and hurt her knees and had been taken to the hospital. The doctor had ordered her to have complete bed rest for at least a week. Leslie even wanted to hire a private nurse to take care of her, but their Auntie Moira, who was visiting the family at the time, wouldn't hear of it.

"I will not allow a stranger to take care of my mother," she had argued, and giving Pollyanna no chance to reply, had stormed out of her sister's home, slamming the front door behind her.

While Clovis remained across Tom's knees, he felt warmth pouring into them and his legs felt strangely stronger than normal. At the same time, he thought how weird the little kitten was! He guessed it must have been the book he had begun reading, which alleviated his boredom and suppressed the urge that came over him, to push Clovis off his lap and to declare how lazy he thought he was.

It's a good thing he was enjoying the story he was reading because they must have sat in the same position for over half an hour before Clovis stirred, and as Tom looked at him, the kitten winked again, then yawned and patted his knees with his two front paws for the second time, before jumping off his lap. Clovis proceeded to stretch his body in different directions, and then he gave a big yawn, flicked his tail up in the air, and stared up at Tom.

Although Clovis' mouth was closed, Tom immediately felt that the kitten was trying to communicate something to him before he walked over to his bowl of water and began to lap it up. Tom had gotten the impression that the kitten had said - *you are all right now* or *something or someone is OK now* - but not in words. Tom called this feeling his crazy notion.

This puzzled him greatly, and he wished that he could share his feelings with someone. He thought of his sister, but knew that he could not confide in her. Lucy was the last person he could say anything to that he wouldn't want all the children in their close neighbourhood to hear about. He did not say anything to his parents either, not until his dad came home the following evening after work and told them his own news.

"Pollyanna," said Leslie, "neither you nor the children are going to believe what I am about to tell you."

Pollyanna, Lucy and Tom, quickly took seats around the kitchen table. Leslie took off his coat and scarf and threw them over the nearest chair, then sat on the seat, unsmiling. The others immediately thought the worst. Without a word, Pollyanna poured a mug of tea from the teapot, which she and the children then passed around the table to Leslie, as if they were playing a game of pass the parcel.

Leslie examined the mug and its contents before gulping down a big mouthful. Tom looked at his father, thinking to himself - I just don't know how anyone can drink tea as hot as my dad, without complaining of a scald mouth.

Leslie said nothing until after he had swallowed his second mouthful of tea. "That tasted good," he told them, and licked his lips. "Better than the poison I get at the office. You know grandma Gertrude was ordered to stay in bed because of the accident?" He looked at his family.

Pollyanna nodded. Lucy had adopted one of her weird facial expressions, and Tom was all ears.

"Well…" Leslie continued, giving the side of his head a quick scratch. Lucy and Tom pulled scornful faces, and their mother looked from her husband to the dining table in disbelief, as tiny white flakes landed on it.

"Have you got dandruff Leslie, or is it dry scalp?" she asked.

Leslie looked as if he had no idea what Pollyanna was asking, but then he casually replied, "Oh, *that*." He had looked down at the table absent-mindedly.

"Not to worry," said Pollyanna rather hurriedly. "What have you got to tell us, about mama?"

"Mmmh, that's what I call a nice cup of tea," was Leslie's response, after draining the mug. "More please, and a couple of biscuits would go nicely with the second mug," he added expectantly. Lucy reached for her father's mug, poured the tea, accidentally spilling a little on the table.

"Leave it, leave it," repeated Pollyanna, rather snappily, looking a little agitated.

Lucy leant backwards, tilting the chair, in order to reach the biscuit tin, which she shoved towards her dad, who helped himself to quite a few. Tom could tell by the looks on his mum's and his sister's faces that they shared his anxiety, waiting for Leslie to make his announcement.

"I saw her, mama Gertrude, shopping in the store, about twenty minutes…. How long have I been sitting here? Let me see…" He looked at his watch, "Ah, the time it took me to drive home, and… must be a good 45 minutes ago." He raised his voice a little, "She seemed perfectly fine to me, no bandaged knees and she was walking unaided without her stick."

"Thank goodness for that!" Pollyanna exclaimed. With the worry gone, she relaxed, and they sat in silence for a moment or two.

"I wonder what doctor Beck was on about," said Pollyanna, breaking the silence. "When I rang the surgery, she distinctly told me that mama needed bed rest." She turned to Leslie. "Darling, you know the rest."

"Yes, I do know. I saw her on the day of the accident, remember? I was the one who was forced to collect her from the hospital," Leslie further reminded, looking as baffled as his wife.

"That doctor was wrong, that's all," said Lucy. "Gran's 'as tough as an old boot.' Isn't that what you always say, dad?"

Neither Leslie nor Pollyanna replied, they stared at each other and shook their heads.

After a moment of two, Pollyanna snapped out of her assumed contemplation. "Mama had X-rays and everything done. Doctor Beck told me that her knees were badly bruised and swollen and that she had been shaking all over. She even suggested that her initial one week of bed rest, might not be enough."

"Well, yes, I know," agreed Leslie, looking even more perplexed.

He stood up, shrugged his shoulders and picked up the newspaper and the mug, which was still half-full of tea. He proceeded to use the newspaper to brush the white flakes from off the table onto the kitchen floor, and then he looked at his wife in a casual manner.

"All right, dear?" he asked, dipping fingers into the biscuit tin. Pollyanna slapped his hand, shook her head and looked at him disapprovingly and then at the floor.

The children sat and watched their father walk out of the kitchen, but then he paused to take a sip of his tea before he walked on again. He was halfway down the hallway when his request came. "Tom! Bring me a few biscuits, will you, and a fresh pot of this good stuff," he added. "I need the warmth and extra energy, so please don't be too sparing with the sugar, and son..."

"Yes, dad!" Tom replied just as loud, in fear that his father had suddenly developed a hearing problem.

"Please come and get me as soon as dinner is ready, I am starving," he announced, a little quieter this time.

"Will do, dad," Tom replied in a softer tone of voice too, looking after him.

Pollyanna placed a fresh pot of tea and a plate with a few biscuits on a tray. "He is only getting two more," she said. "We don't want to spoil his appetite just before dinner."

"Don't be so stingy, mum," said Lucy.

With his sister, there was no telling whether she was joking when she said certain things. Pollyanna laughed all the same, but Tom didn't.

Lucy offered to take the tray to her dad, so Tom walked out of the kitchen and into the living room where Clovis sat scratching his belly.

The kitten rubbed his head before he proceeded to give his body a good clean all over, after which he turned and looked up at Tom, who jokingly asked him whether he would like him to wash the parts he could not reach. To Tom's great astonishment, Clovis stopped licking himself, stared up at him and shook his head.

No thank you, Tom, I can manage - was what he heard.

Clovis held his gaze for a short time. In the pit of Tom's stomach, was another crazy notion, but this time he felt that the kitten had asked - *Why are you looking so amazed?* - He then began to chase his tail, around and around he ran. When he had caught his tail in his mouth, he stopped and looked up at Tom again. Tom was smiling at him. He let go off his tail and meowed, then he walked over to join Lady H, and Zack. The mother cat was stretched out on her belly. Clovis lay with his head and two front paws on her, and Zack stood looking at them, as if he didn't really belong.

It wasn't long afterwards that Pollyanna walked into the room and sat down next to Tom. "Thank goodness, I can be out of that kitchen, give my poor tired feet a few minutes rest." Her faint smile vanished as she noticed Tom's puzzled expression. "What is it that is of such concern to you, son? You look really perplexed?"

Tom plucked up the courage and told his mother what had happened the day before. Pollyanna said nothing at first. She looked at him, then at Clovis, coughed, and then stood up, and in a controlled manner, she said, "I hope, Tom, you are not suggesting what I think you are suggesting."

Tom nodded.

"You are?" she asked.

"Yes," he replied, casually.

"Never," she said, in a low deep voice. She took a few steps backwards, looking astonished. "You are kidding me. That could never happen, not in a million years," she added disbelievingly.

"No, and why not?" asked Tom. "Wasn't it you who told me to believe that unusual things do and can happen, mum?" he asked wryly.

Pollyanna stared at him, as if she was at a loss for words, and so Tom continued, "You told me that I should believe and have faith," he said.

"Yes, but, you are asking me to believe that this little kitten, who two months ago we nearly lost. Do you remember?" she asked, frowning.

"Yes, but...."

82

"Do not 'yes but' me, Tom." Pollyanna had raised her voice. "How can a little kitten, this cat, any animal for that matter, heal anyone? Answer me that." She looked at Tom like a doctor looking at a patient. "He is an animal, for goodness sake," she said warily, touching her forehead. "Are you sure you are feeling yourself today, son?" she asked.

Tom responded without blinking, "My nana has been healed!" he cried.

"Look here Tom," retorted Pollyanna, raising her voice too, "I have heard some strange stories, but yours tops them all. You must admit you have been coming home with a few quirky tales over the last few months, which I have tolerated, but you are beginning to test the extent of my patience. This new belief of yours is taking it much too far."

Tom, defensively replied, "Nana Gertrude was healed from a distance, however quirky it may sound, and I believe that Clovis had something to do with it." He was conscious that he had raised his voice, but he didn't care much because he felt disappointed. "I told you what happened and I believe there can be no other explanation. It's just too much of a coincidence. How else could nana have gotten better so quickly?"

In the heat of the moment, Tom glanced over at Clovis and noticed that the kitten was watching them, and that his eyes appeared to be larger than normal, and the colour had changed, they appeared green instead of their usual yellowish colour.

"I don't yet know the answer, as to why mama has gotten better so quickly, but I can say this, your suggestion sounds quite ludicrous, simply impossible."

Tom fell silent. Any thought he might have had of letting his mother know about Clovis' other magical capabilities left him, for fear his mother might just decide to have him put into a straightjacket and sent to a loony bin.

Pollyanna looked briefly into her son's eyes without speaking. When she did speak again, she sounded gentler.

"Until I see this cat," she said, pointing at Clovis.

Clovis turned again and looked up at Pollyanna, but this time his eyes had changed back to their usual colour. The kitten shook his head and grunted heavily, so that even Pollyanna looked over at him in surprise, before he turned back and rested his head on his mother.

"Until I see Clovis, actually doing something miraculous or magical, which is never going to happen, I do not believe and cannot accept that he healed mama. The very thought sounds barmy. The idea is, well, it's simply unthinkable."

She then mumbled something, which Tom could not make out, and he didn't ask her to repeat before she spoke again, "I would be unfit to practise in my profession and furthermore, I would also be fit for a loony bin, if I believed that..." Pollyanna paused, shook her head again and looked at Tom, with a serious expression on her face. "Son, none of what you have said to me makes any sense. Please do not go around telling your friends what you have just told me," she further advised. "I have never heard such a silly notion in my life. Come on now, think about it, it really does sound quite ludicrous."

"Mum," Tom retorted impatiently, "You are beginning to sound like Craig. That is the second time you have used that word, which I don't understand."

"Ludicrous in your case means unreasonable, completely silly, absurd and impractical." Pollyanna then took a quick breath, which she exhaled just as quickly. "Tom," she continued, "what I mean to say is, you are putting forward fantastic suggestions to me, which I just cannot agree with."

"Impossible to you mother, but not to me, I believe that Clovis had something to do with nana Gertrude's knees getting better overnight. Just like I haven't forgotten that Carl's sister, Gula, played a part in Clovis' healing, right in this room." Tom sounded cross.

Pollyanna said nothing more. Instead, she took his head in her hands and, before kissing it, she rubbed it all over, which he painfully tolerated, due to the fact that he had to re-comb his hair. Afterwards, Pollyanna got up and walking out of the room, she said, "Dinner won't be long now. I had better go and see how that sister of yours is getting on with laying the table."

Tom nodded, remembering that it was at times like these when his mother would jokingly call him, 'hard headed', but she didn't, not this time, she had said a lot of other things in its place, which made him feel a lot worse.

After she left the room, Clovis looked up at Tom, and once again his inkling told him that the young cat was Saying - *Tom, be patient with your mother, and give her time, she'll come round.*

Chapter Eight

Taking a Stand

For the rest of that weekend, Tom found things to do outside. And during meal times, he even asked to be allowed to eat in his room or in the study. He was doing his best to avoid his mother, and the following Monday wasn't a good day for him at school either, he was feeling really miserable.

He spent the whole day going over in his mind the argument he had with his mother, and occasionally he nursed his churning stomach. He looked so miserable that not even his closest friends seemed able to change his mood. This sadness seemed to have rubbed off on Carl, because he took one look at Tom, and his sulking cap went on too, even though he didn't even bother to ask his friend, what was troubling him. Or perhaps he didn't need to.

The climax came in the last lesson of the day, during Mr Fred Mooney's science class. Carl sat musing over how well some people's names seem to suit them, using his science teacher's name, as a prime example. The teacher's face and head reminded him of pictures he had seen in children's books, of a man in the moon.

This particular teacher wasn't one of the children's favourites. In fact, so far, Carl could not help but wonder whether the majority of the children in his year group, admired any other teacher in the school besides Mrs Townsend, their religious education teacher.

This was Year 6's last year at St Catharine's Primary School, before they would begin their first year at St Jacoby's Secondary High, after the impending summer holiday. Neither Carl nor any of his close friends had ever been given detention. They had not gotten themselves into any trouble – until this particular afternoon.

"Over the course of our last term," Mr Mooney announced, "we are going to carry out a number of experiments, to get you all in the swing of things for when you move on to secondary school."

He grinned and almost lost his top denture, but quickly pushed it back in place. Most of the children sniggered and grimaced, except for Carl, Mary, Tom and Nikhil.

"Now then," continued the teacher, who had raised his voice above the noisy confusion that had begun the minute he started talking. "Before I continue I would like silence in my classroom. That means you too, Gaia Cartwright. You and your brother are not identical, so I'm hoping that your behaviour will be nothing like his." Gaia looked at Trevor, then back at the teacher, but did not respond to the teacher's comment. The teacher fidgeted a little, and disinterestedly, many of the children continued chattering and laughing together. A few even banged on their desks, and two girls began to throw bits of screwed-up paper at each other and across the room towards the litter bin.

Mr Mooney raised his voice, "If the noise continues, and if one more piece of paper is thrown across this classroom, everyone will be detained after this lesson." His announcement brought about silence. "Now then that's better," he said. "This afternoon, I am going to show you the heart of an animal, and not only would I like you to have a guess at what animal it came from, but I will be dissecting it and we'll discuss it."

"*Dissecting* an animal's heart," cried Luke Reid, crossing his legs.

"Uncross those legs in my classroom!" ordered the teacher.

"What do you mean, Sir?" asked Luke, uncrossing his legs and grinning.

"And you can wipe that stupid grin off your face," demanded the teacher. "What I've just said is what I mean. I am going to cut open this heart and examine it." He held up the heart and jiggled it about as if it were a bell, with a stern expression on his face.

"How wicked!" exclaimed Naomi Jones, turning away, looking squeamish, and paler than normal.

"I really don't like the idea of that," said Gaia, disapprovingly.

There followed an outburst of unsavoury remarks, after Kara Buckling bellowed, "Disgusting!"

Sean Scully whispered, "Not me, weirdo."

"How horrid!" cried Omotayo.

After that, the teacher was likened to a nerd, and many other unpleasant names. Craig and Luke, however, were very keen to take part in the teacher's experiment. They stood up.

"Yes," chorused Craig and Luke together, each shaking a hand in the air and bobbing about, as they began to sing and to dance. "That's the way, aha, aha, we like it," they exclaimed a couple of times, grinning as they attempted to do 'the bump'. Afterwards they smacked hands together and giggled loudly.

"Sit down immediately, you two!" cried the teacher, looking annoyed.

"Will I have a chance to do one, Mr Mooney?" asked Craig.

"Me too," cried Luke. "I would like to cut one open."

"Yes, yes all right. Sit, sit back in your seats," stuttered the teacher in growing irritation, as the commotion continued. "I have about six, so after I have shown you how it's done, you can all form yourselves into groups and do your own," he told them in a high-pitched tone of voice. "Remember to make notes because I will expect a write-up afterwards."

"Will we be frying them on the Bunsen burner afterwards, Sir?" asked Claude Lamoure, a new French boy, who acted as though he was the least able in the science lessons, when in fact he always managed to get top marks.

"And why would we do that, Claude?" asked the teacher, in growing frustration.

"Oh, sorry Sir, I thought that's why you are going to cut it up," replied Claude, in fake innocence.

Most of the children thought Claude funny and began to giggle again, until Tom's hand went up, instantly the class went quiet.

"About time," said the teacher – Yes, Tom?"

"Can I be excused from this particular lesson, Sir?"

"Me too," joined Carl, in his usual quiet voice.

"And me too, Sir," put in Mary, with her hand up.

Nikhil, joined in. "If you don't mind, Sir, I would also like to be excused from the lesson."

"I see," said the teacher. "Would anyone else like to join these four?" he asked, looking around the classroom.

Naomi and Gaia looked at each other and shrugged.

No one answered.

"You four, before I decide whether I should grant your request, I need to know why you have asked to leave my lesson," said the teacher.

"Well, Sir, I can only speak for myself when I say I don't approve of anyone dissecting animals, or any part of any animal of any kind for any reason," said Tom.

"I am of the same opinion, Sir," said Carl in agreement, adding, "so, if you don't mind Mr Mooney, I prefer not to be present when *any* of it is taking place."

Carl had stressed the word 'any' and it caused the teacher to look over at him, showing surprise.

"As far as I am concerned," said Mary, "that is as good as killing the animal. My parents and I don't approve of anything like what you are about to do, Sir." Mary looked as if she had just received the shock of her young life.

Nikhil joined in, "A lot of animals are sacred in my religion, and so we do not kill animals, unless it is for ritualistic purposes, and then it is done by a special person. For example, we believe that the cow is a sacred animal, so we would never slaughter a cow," he added. "My family, not just my immediate family, I believe all my relatives are vegetarians."

"Is that so, Nikhil?" asked the teacher.

Nikhil replied, "Yes, Sir, that is exactly so."

"I see," said the teacher. "Most interesting," he added, and then asked, "What about you three?" He looked expressly at Carl. "Do any of you eat meat of any kind?" The teacher then looked at Mary and Tom.

"I already said, my parents and I, we are vegetarians," replied Mary.

"Very well, in that case, Nikhil, and you three, may leave my class," announced the teacher, waving his hand dismissively towards the classroom door. "Please return at the end of this lesson for detention. You will explain to me, in no less than 20 lines each, why you refused to remain in this lesson today. This you will take to the head teacher, after I have read them. I will also be giving each of you a note to take home to your parents," he added.

Carl's hand went up.

"Yes, Carl," said Mr Mooney, flatly.

All heads now turned in Carl's direction.

"What do you have to say for yourself, young McKenzie? Let's hope you have had a change of mind."

Carl replied boldly, "Oh no, Sir, I haven't changed my mind. I wouldn't. I simply wanted to say, you need to inform my parents before you keep me behind after school, Sir. I am sure you wouldn't have forgotten."

"Is that so?"

"Yes, Sir, I'm afraid that is so. My parents sent a letter last year, and I believe that the head teacher thought it a good idea, and has adopted it for all children in the school."

"Is that so, Carl?" asked the teacher.

"Yes, I believe so, Sir," replied Carl, bravely. "It was announced in assembly, just before we broke up for the Christmas holiday last year. Were you away, Sir?"

"What utter nonsense," the teacher replied. "Right, Carl, Mary, Tom and you, Nikhil, will follow me to Mr Railways' office." He heaved his chest. "We will sort this… The rest of you can get on by reading page 17 in your textbooks." He waved dismissively again. "And don't think you are going to sit here and chatter unproductively while I am out of this classroom because, I shall be asking all of you about what you have read, on my return." Mr Mooney stormed out of the room, adding, and "Come along, you four." Then he muttered, "Utter baloney."

The teacher bumbled briskly ahead of his four pupils along the unusually long lit corridor, which led to the head teacher's office. Now and again, he turned, "Stop slouching and walk up straight now," he snapped. "And stop lagging behind. You won't worm yourselves out of this one. Hurry up, I have a lesson to get back to," he reminded.

As they reached the head teachers' office, the door was closed. Mr Mooney paused to wipe sweat from his face with a soiled handkerchief, before knocking.

"You may enter," said the pleasant-sounding voice of the head teacher; a thin-faced, plain-looking gentleman in his early fifties, dressed in a dark-brown suit, and seated behind a thick old-fashioned-looking wooden desk. He looked up from behind the pile of papers before him. "Um-ah, Mr Mooney," he said cheerfully, as he leant sideways to look from the teacher to the four children. "Don't tell me, Tom, Carl, Nockhill..."

"*Nikhil*, Sir," corrected Nikhil, his face brightening.

"Yes, so it is, *Nikhil*, and you too Mary Stuart. This is a first. What have you four been up to?" he asked, secretly amused, as his glance left the children to look at their teacher. "Well, Mr Mooney, you have brought them before me, what have they been up to?"

"These four," began the teacher rather loudly, as if he was still in his classroom, "have asked, politely mind you, to be excused from my lesson."

"That's a first too," said the head teacher, the smile leaving his face. "Why is that, Carl?" he asked.

"Sir, I would not be able to stomach seeing the heart of a dead animal cut up and examined. I would be sickened by it, Sir."

"I see. And I suppose it is the same for the rest of you?" assumed the head teacher, looking from Nikhil to Tom, and then at Mary, who blushed.

"Not quite Sir," remarked Tom.

"That's right," agreed Nikhil.

"That's right," repeated the head teacher. "Are you saying that you feel the same way, Nikhil?"

"Well, Sir, I have given my reasons to Mr Mooney," replied Nikhil, boldly.

"And what reason did you give, Nikhil? I would like to hear it."

"We Hindus do not take the killing of an animal as a joke. Some are quite sacred to us, Sir," replied Nikhil.

"Yes, I do remember." Mr Railways responded gently, "I am familiar with your beliefs and customs. I was brought up in India you know. You are right to ask to be excused. In fact, none of you have ever given cause to be brought before me in the past, certainly not for any reason such as this. What do you have to say for yourself, Tom?"

"I feel the same as Carl," replied Tom.

"Also," put in Mr Mooney, "Carl was impertinent enough to remind me that you have announced and given out letters to the effect that pupils will not be detained after school, unless their parents have first been informed. I did not believe it for a minute. The impudence of this boy," said the teacher.

"Carl, and the rest of you, please wait outside my office," ordered Mr Railways.

As the youngsters left, closing the door behind them, the head teacher turned to Mr Mooney, and in a soft voice he said, "Not impudence at all Fred. Carl is quite right. Where were you when I announced my decision? You must have been taking one of your many days off, no doubt."

Mr Mooney's face went pale.

"I think that you should excuse these four pupils from your lesson today, Fred, don't you?"

Mr Mooney attempted a slight bow of the head.

"I hope you are not going to suggest that they should write lines either," said the head teacher, looking directly at Mr Mooney, who looked towards the floor. "Lines," he replied nervously, "Oh no, good heavens, Mr Railways, not at all."

"I think they should spend the rest of the lesson in the library, don't you?" asked the head teacher.

"Yes, good idea," replied Mr Mooney, in false enthusiasm, opening the door quickly. "Go ahead, you four, to the library for the rest of the lesson, and be quick about it," he ordered half-heartedly.

The children walked away, whispering and smiling happily with each another.

Mr Railways called their teacher back. "A quick word before you go, Fred. Try not to be too hard on those four children. Beside the fact that they are four of our brightest and best-behaved pupils in this school, their parents contribute handsomely to the school funds."

"Oh, I see, yes, well all right," said Mr Mooney, giving a false smile and stepping backwards, edging his way towards the door and opening it again. "I understand Samuel. If that is all, I must return to the rest of the class, see what they are up to." This time he bowed properly.

Mr Mooney hurried away, leaving the head teacher's door ajar. He rushed along the corridor, occasionally pausing to wipe sweat from his face. As he reached the door to his classroom, he paused again for the sixth time. With an ear close to the door, he undid the buttons on the grey and black striped ill-fitting jacket he was wearing before he entered.

Chapter Nine

At the Festival

The last Saturday in the month of June was a glorious day, the sun was unusually hot. Carl, Tom and the rest of their friends had just arrived at the local summer festival that was being held in the grounds of a large old mansion house, which was a good walking distance from their homes. This cultural event was organised by a group of local people who called themselves the 'Neighbourhood Friends'. They had received sponsorship from the local borough council and other private organisations. This festival had been taking place quite successfully, and was in its third successive year.

As the children neared the main entrance, they could not avoid the oddly dressed couple standing on the pavement, playfully handing out candyfloss. Carl and Tom looked at each other and fell back a few paces from the others to have a private conversation.

"Strange," said Carl.

"Sure is," agreed Tom.

They looked reproachfully and shook their heads at the two ghoulish-looking adults, who practically thrust a candyfloss each towards them.

The two boys couldn't help noticing that the children who accepted the candyfloss looked as if they were mesmerised by the couple. The main man reached inside a wooden keg and produced the candyfloss, but on inspection, Carl and Tom realised that the barrel was empty. The man grinned. "Mystery and magic," he said, and then released a loud clown-like laughter, which amused and attracted even more youngsters to them.

"How funny," remarked Mary. "What can be so good about eating candyfloss? Too much sugar rots the teeth," she whispered, as she watched kids breaking and biting ravenously at the candyfloss, which seemed never-ending on the sticks in their hands.

"No thank you, I want to eat food, not candyfloss," Craig remarked rather rudely, as the weird-looking woman shoved a stick of pink-coloured candyfloss towards him. Each time the man pushed his hand into the barrel, he produced a stick full of a different coloured candyfloss. Looking more and more delighted, he giggled hilariously as he handed a stick of candyfloss to the next child waiting eagerly and excitedly. A little further on, two other couples busied themselves handing out more candyfloss. Carl and Tom looked questioningly at each other again, but said nothing. The rest of their friends were already a step or two head of them.

One person in particular stood out because he was the largest and bulkiest of the lot. He was dressed in a three-quarter-length grey coat that matched the rest of his odd-looking clothes. He looked quite shapeless and clown-like, especially his large face, which looked as white as snow. He wore an excessively large square-shaped hat, and big, long square-shaped shoes. It was evident that the children believed them to be clowns, from the way they looked and by their actions. Carl and Tom thought differently.

"Tom," said Carl, "I wonder, is that weirdo really a clown or could it be that he's in disguise?"

"There was something about those people back there that I didn't like either, especially the big man," said Tom, in agreement, as they continued walking towards a larger crowd of people who were all dressed-up and looking happy.

"You are right, *really unnerving*, and that large man,

there's something quite detestable about him," suggested Carl.

"Yes," Tom agreed, "I got that same feeling too."

Instinctively, the two friends turned, only to realise that the man they though most queer was looking intently at them. He snarled loudly, and the children who had gathered around jumped about delightedly on the spot, eagerly waiting their turn to get a stick of candyfloss and giggling enthusiastically.

The festivities were arranged not only outside, but also inside the mansion, which was now mostly used as offices by the local council. The great hall, which was normally used for occasions such as wedding receptions and other important functions, was the main area used to display certain very important objects.

As the friends advanced further into the hall, they overheard a couple, dressed like hippies, talking. They had evidently visited a certain room on the top floor of this great house and felt sure that it was haunted. The woman swore she had seen a ghost walking around, but couldn't tell whether the apparition was male or female, only that it kept on appearing and disappearing, and that it appeared to be anxious, as if searching for something or someone.

Most of the friends had giggled quietly, but not Mary, she hesitated nervously and looked quite frightened because she was superstitious and believed in spirits. Mary's first urge was to turn back and wait outside for her friends, but she didn't because she didn't want to miss out on anything, so she made sure she placed herself between Carl and Tom, where she felt safest as they walked along.

"Thank goodness my sister is not here," Carl announced as they left the great hall and entered another room.

"Why?" asked Nikhil, a broad smile enhancing his already attractive features.

"My sister believes in ghosts so if she was here, she would have seen them, and what followed next would have been most embarrassing for me."

"Why is that?" asked Mary.

Carl began to explain. "You don't know my sister like I do," he told them. "She would begin one of her 'sending to the light' notions."

"Oh?" interrupted Mary.

"Yes, oh," remarked Carl. "Encouraging the spirits to walk into the light, this would enable them to leave the house that they are haunting. She'd call on God knows how many angels, and mumble whatever else comes to her at the time, including their names and other things that only they or someone who knew them could possibly know about."

"Goodness," said Mary, clearly intrigued. "Your sister is like that?"

Carl chuckled.

"And where would she be asking them go?" asked Nikhil, looking curious.

"The Spirit World," replied Carl, looking a little pensive.

"I like Gula," Nikhil admitted. "I think she's a noble girl. Sometimes I get this uncanny feeling that she's not of this world," he added, to the surprise of the rest of his friends. Carl looked at Nikhil, disguising the fact that he understood him, but said nothing.

The room they entered was much larger than the main entrance hall. It was being used to exhibit a lot of artwork, including sculptures, paintings, exquisite looking traditional forms of dress and jewellery from many countries of the world.

Carl looked rather curious when he saw that there were more statues of people of ancient times, and showed particular interest at first, in those from Egypt.

"I can't wait to visit Egypt now. My parents changed their minds about Egypt and took us to Spain," he told them.

The others smiled at him. They were remembering what he had said in their Religious Education class months earlier, when they were discussing other countries. He had said that he didn't fancy visiting Egypt. Suddenly a subtle change took Carl by surprise as he stood staring at the statue of an Egyptian person of obvious nobility.

This went unnoticed by Tom, until they left the room, when he was suddenly struck by the likeness of the male statue's features, to those of his friend. In fact, it was so uncanny that he felt they might have been twins, had it been in this lifetime. Tom decided not to make his thoughts known to the others, at least not yet. He understood then why Carl had quickly walked away from it. It must have been quite unnerving for him.

They had paused briefly to admire some old jewellery on display in a long glass cabinet before they entered the adjoining room. This was a lively room, which was decorated and furnished with items from the Elizabethan era. Many people had gathered there, all dressed in different costumes from that period. The friends soon realised that there were various competitions going on. The only competition that interested Tom, was the prize to any male over ten years of age who could imitate a famous singer, by singing at least a verse of one of his many songs.

After he read the poster, Tom joked with his friends. "Luckily, it's not that bloke's look-alike they are asking for," he said, pointing to a man selling raffle tickets. "No one could look like that guy, unless they had plastic surgery."

Everyone shared the joke, to the extent that their laughter had attracted the attention of quite a few people nearby and had encouraged smiles and laughter around the room.

It cost a pound to enter the competition, but the prize was a secret, so Tom decided not to enter, as he didn't like the idea of it being a surprise. He learnt much later on that the prize was to meet and to dine out with the famous singer and his family, and the winner would also receive his latest signed album, which would have been something. Tom was disappointed to have missed the chance to win this prize.

Nikhil suggested that they should visit the haunted

room upstairs, but Mary, looking quite frightened, nervously objected to the idea. As it ended up being a split decision, Carl and Tom also decided against the journey upstairs, which greatly pleased Mary and brought her back to her usual lively self.

A group of about six kids walked past them holding sticks of candyfloss. By the sound of their laughter and chatter, they were happily exploring the great house. The six children got to the last section of the building and entered a downstairs gym. They played on the exercise equipment for a while, but soon got bored and walked through into the last downstairs room.

Apart from what looked like an empty swimming pool, the room was otherwise bare. All but one young girl entered the empty pool and began to play at pretend swimming and splashing each other. The young girl who did not join in the fun, sat at the edge of the pool watching and laughing excitedly with them. They became so engrossed in their pretend play and lost all recollection that the pool was empty when they first entered, because the pool was enchanted. They did not realise that the pool was slowly filling up with water, until the young girl outside the pool noticed and shouted out to them, but by then, they were up to their knees in the enchanted water.

Terrified, they began to scream and tried to scramble out of the pool, which was now filling up at a rapid speed, and before they knew it, the water was at their waists and turned into what looked like a whirlpool from which they could not escape. Frantic, the young girl jumped up from where she sat and began to scream and shout at them to get out of the pool.

Petrified, she ran towards the door to leave the room. Suddenly, the room went dark and she froze momentarily on the spot. With shaky hands, she fumbled until she found the door handle, and after great effort she managed to open the door. She began to call out and to scream as loudly as she could for help, but no one heard her. The darkness left the room as suddenly as it had appeared. Anxious, she turned and looked towards the pool. To her horror, she saw that the pool was empty and her companions were nowhere in sight. She dashed through the door and ran crying, "They've gone, the pool, they've gone," until she was back in the crowded room.

A crowd gathered around her as she threw herself onto the floor, she was shaking and whimpering and speaking what they thought was gibberish. She became quite uncontrollable for some time, until a woman coaxed her into drinking some water. This seemed to calm her and enabled her to relate her story about what had taken place.

Someone called the police while the security staff searched the great house from room to room, until they got to the last room with the empty swimming pool. They stared in disbelief and puzzlement at the empty dry pool and then at the young girl who had told them her story.

"I tell you, we were all together," she cried. "I didn't go in, but Sam did, and Elle, Richard, Tamzin, and-and Paul, they are my friends, they were in the pool, and now they are gone. You have got to believe me, they are all gone." Her voice trailed away towards the end of her speech, and her body sank onto the floor once more, she looked shocked and exhausted.

"What's your name little one?" asked a kind looking woman who had stooped down next to her.

"My name is, Tanika," the young girl replied in almost a whisper.

"Tanika," repeated the woman, "that's a real pretty name – Tanika, you said the room went dark." The girl nodded her head. "They must have played a trick on you, and sneaked out and left you alone, while it was still dark. It must have been one of them who turned the light off," suggested the woman in a soft friendly voice.

The girl cried out again, but her voice was weaker than before, "No, no, please listen to me. They couldn't, they couldn't get out," she sobbed, "not without me. I was standing by the door, feeling for the handle, to open it. When it got light again, I looked for them, but-but, they were gone. Listen, you must believe me, I'm speaking the truth." She had whimpered her last few words.

Carl and his friends did not hear what had happened because they had left the building before the confusion. Outside, there were spectacular events taking place, with lots of children's amusements, including donkey and pony rides and a small circus. The friends stopped and watched two clowns on tall stilts, grinning and walking around telling jokes.

A bunch of youngsters laughed out loud at a couple who were dressed up, acting like kangaroos. Two ponies pulled a low carriage, which was supported by two of the largest old-fashioned wheels they had only ever seen in old books and magazines or at the museum. A few kids sat in an old-fashioned horse and carriage with their parents, waiting for the driver to move off. A girl and a boy sat smiling happily on a pair of donkeys, obviously enjoying their rides, on quite a long improvised-looking track.

The streets used for the occasion were blocked off from traffic and were festooned with balloons, streamers, coloured lights and other decorations. Flags representing many different countries of the world were also on display high in the air. The British flag was impossible to miss. It was enormous and flew high up in the air like a kite.

A group of people were masquerading and dancing to music. Tom especially liked the calypso band. Elsewhere, a bunch of teenage girls and boys were dancing to hip-hop music. As they neared a group of ballet dancers, Craig laughed saying, "I don't like ballet," and pointed rudely at the male ballet dancers who were dancing to swan lake.

The others, embarrassed by Craig, walked away from him so that he had to run to catch up with them. They had stopped to watch a puppet show with a group of children who were seated on the ground, laughing and talking happily.

The face-painting was popular, and youngsters flocked the stalls selling hot dogs and patties. Carl and Tom loved the hot chilli patties. They bought two each and made a fifty pence bet with each other, as to who would finish eating the quickest. Remarkably enough, Tom won. They both ended up with hiccups, which only eased a little after they drank almost a whole bottle of mineral water each. After seeing all they felt they wanted to see, the group of friends left the festival, laughing and joking about their favourite events.

Chapter Ten

Food for Thought

The friends had planned to have an Indian meal after the festival. As they walked along the busy high street leading to the restaurant, which was chosen by Craig, he began to complain that he had not eaten breakfast that morning, and it was well past lunchtime. He had been adamant that he didn't fancy buying anything from the many food stalls at the festival. He had complained that there were flies everywhere, which was really a gross exaggeration on his part.

Nikhil stopped in his tracks, as a cat walking along the road, stopped and looked up at him. The others stopped too, wondering why Nikhil had stopped so abruptly. Nikhil watched the cat until it disappeared out of sight.

"Watching that cat, made me think about you Carl," he said at length. "And I feel sad for you because, I know how much you would like to take that kitten home."

"That's right. His name is Clovis," said Tom, agreeing with Nikhil.

Carl sighed and Nikhil continued. "My parents don't like cats. They don't like any pets at all. My sister and I, we begged and begged for weeks for a little puppy, once, but they wouldn't let us have him."

"Goodness!" cried Mary, a hand on the spot where she supposed her heart to be.

"But I will help," said Nikhil, supportively. "I will ask Vishnu, Lakshmi, and Hanuman, all three of them, for help," he announced cheerfully, looking proud.

"Who are they, relatives of yours Nikhil?" asked Mary, looking puzzled.

Nikhil giggled a little.

"No, Vishnu is our great Hindu god, and Lakshmi is one of our goddesses."

"Oh," said Mary, looking surprised, "I had no idea there was more than one god or that there are actually gods and goddesses living in India. We only have a queen and her husband, the duke, but the queen is the head of the throne of England, Scotland and Wales you know." Mary sounded proud.

"I know that Mary," Nikhil replied. "The gods and goddesses are not actually there, in India, to be seen. We have gods and goddesses whom we pray to for various reasons," Nikhil informed them brightly.

"That's good," said Carl. "Thanks for offering, Nikhil."

"Yeah mate that sounds *just* great," said Craig, looking bored until Mary asked, "What do they do these gods and goddesses?"

"Nothing I expect," Craig interrupted. He pulled at the chewing gum in his mouth, slurped and dribbled down the front of his shirt.

"Yuck, how *disgusting*," said Mary.

Ignoring her, Craig wiped his hands on his clothes, "They are just mythical characters. Every religion has them. They are no different from the Egyptian goddess Bastet, Mrs Townsend told us about in class," he reminded them.

Nikhil blushed. "They are not mythical," he said. "It is no different to you believing in Jesus."

"I never said I did," argued Craig.

Mary gave Craig a warning glance, which he blatantly ignored.

"Take no notice of him Nikhil," she said, with a dismissive sweeping hand gesture. "The rest of us would like to hear, *wouldn't we*?" The other boys looked from Mary to Nikhil in silence.

"Go on Nikhil, carry on," she encouraged, in a commanding tone of voice.

"Well, Lakshmi means good luck to us Hindus."

"Oh," said Mary, interrupting and looking surprised again.

"Yes," Nikhil added brightly, "I am a Hindu. Weren't you listening to our teacher? I practise the Indian religion of Hinduism. Hindus believe that it is the main religion of India and also the oldest of the worldwide religions."

"What!" yelled Craig, "That's rubbish - nonsense, as my father would say."

"No, it's not rubbish," cried Nikhil, defensively, looking a little irritated.

"Don't listen to him Nikhil," said Carl. "Craig is just ignorant of certain things. Perhaps he's not as knowledgeable as he makes out. Besides, we are not here to get into a religious debate because of you, Craig."

"If he's not ignorant, he's being prejudice," put in Mary, giving Craig a withering look. "Please stop interrupting," she scolded.

Nikhil tried to continue as if Craig was no longer in their company.

"That is what my parents taught me. I didn't want to say anything when Mrs Townsend mentioned about reincarnation, but that's what I can't quite understand," Nikhil admitted. "My parents don't even know that I don't get the reincarnation bit of our beliefs because, I haven't said anything to them about my feelings, I'm afraid they might think me stupid."

Craig pulled a face, which the others didn't like, but they continued to ignore him.

"I don't understand," Nikhil repeated again, his eyebrows knitting up.

"What don't you understand about reincarnation?" asked Mary.

Craig sniggered and turned away.

"Reincarnation means that you die and come back again, but not necessarily as the person you were before, I think," said Carl.

"That, I do not believe," said Craig.

The others looked at him questioningly.

"I am not saying that I don't believe in the meaning," he explained. "I mean, I do not believe that when people die they can actually be reborn. I believe that we only live once."

"You definitely won't like the title of the James Bond movie, and you are such a fan," said Tom. They looked oddly at him.

"'You Only Live Twice.' Haven't you seen it?" he asked. "My dad took me to see it. He told me it's a remake. It's a great film."

Anyway, Mrs Townsend said that she would discuss Hinduism more fully with us, next Friday," Nikhil added.

"Yes so she did," put in Craig, sounding uninterested. "There will be no need for her to tell us anything," he continued grumpily, "since we are already having our lesson from a pupil, out here on the street, when all I came here for is a chicken vindaloo with basmati rice, sag aloo and a blooming coke to wash it down with. I would have thought that this discussion could continue nicely over the meal we all agreed to have in this restaurant, or preferably not at all. I am starving." Craig looked annoyed, as he pointed to the tandoori restaurant in front of them, "That, at least, would be the practical and courteous thing to do," he told them.

"How can you eat that stuff?" remarked Carl. "Vindaloo, it's so hot," he declared. "I tasted my dad's once, he loves to cook hot Indian curry. Never again! Ever since that day I've stuck with the curry my mum makes, they are much milder and they taste much better too because, the milder curries bring out the flavour more."

"My mum puts raisins in her curry, and just a *small* amount of pepper," said Mary.

"Couldn't we continue all this around the dining table, please?" Craig begged. But once again the others ignored him.

"Nikhil," asked Mary, "what were you saying about the Indian god and goddess?"

"No, *not again*," Craig stressed.

"Oh yes," said Nikhil, sounding a little more cheerful. "The goddess, Lakshmi, she is known as the goddess of prosperity and wealth. At home we have a shrine in her honour, and we do special rituals for her. She has lots of hands. I can't remember how many exactly, so I won't guess."

Mary looked doubtful.

"And lots of heads," interrupted Craig, then he giggled naughtily. "She sounds like the serpent woman with lots of hands and heads."

"You are talking about Medusa, nitwit," said Tom.

"Yep," replied Craig.

"She is the woman with lots of snakes on her head, not lots of hands and heads, Craig," corrected Carl.

"That is who she sounds like to me," said Craig.

"She does, doesn't she?" suggested Mary, in agreement, and her nose twitched as if she was about to sneeze. "It all sounds nice though," she added quickly, noticing that Nikhil looked offended.

"Yeah, interesting," said Carl. "I wouldn't mind seeing the shrine," he added.

"In that case, you must come to my house Carl," said Nikhil, sounding pleased. "What was I saying? Oh yes, Lakshmi is a mother goddess, so we Indians call her Mata, which means 'mother' in our language, and sometimes she is called Devi, which means goddess," Nikhil further informed them. "Her four arms mean things too… Ah, I remember now, I think Lakshmi has four hands," added Nikhil, with a smile. "My mum's favourite goddess, she is called Kali-Ma or Durga. She is one of the most favourite goddesses in India, but she is not *my* favourite."

"And why is that?" asked Mary.

Nikhil did not reply to Mary's question, instead he blinked at her. "I won't say much about her," he continued, "except that in one of her forms, I can't remember which though, she destroys demons and devils."

"Did you hear that Craig?" asked Carl. "You had better stop being a little devil."

They all laughed.

"There is a mantra I like that my parents often sing to Kali."

Mary beamed with excitement. "Do you know it Nikhil? Sing it to us, please," she begged.

Nikhil shook his head.

"Yeah, go on, I wouldn't mind hearing it," prompted Craig, giving a sly smile.

They knew Craig was being insincere so they turned their backs on him.

"I would like to hear it," said Carl, and Tom, nodded his interest.

Nikhil looked bashful. "Nah, not today, certainly not out here on the street. Perhaps another time, when you visit me at my home, perhaps I'll sing then."

"We are holding you to your promise Nikhil," said Carl.

Nikhil grinned.

"I didn't hear him promise anything," put in Craig.

Put a sock in it!" cried Tom, looking agitated.

"We have pujas, too," Nikhil added quickly.

"What are they," asked Carl, looking interested.

"Sort of worship, like you pray to Mary, we say mantras to Lakshmi for different things, and we can invite our friends. There is a special full moon night when we offer up prayers to her, for blessings. We believe that on this particular night, the goddess visits our home."

"You see her?" asked Mary, showing surprise. "Gosh, your family must be important, sounds as amazing as receiving an invite from the queen."

Nikhil smiled warmly at Mary. "No, she is unseen. At least I think she is. Perhaps important people can see her, but I can't."

"What a shame she's a ghost," teased Craig. Mary suddenly looked a little unnerved.

"That is when she is able to bless us with wealth, my mum said," continued Nikhil.

"In that case, I'm up for it," said Craig.

Once again he was frowned on because no one took him seriously.

"I don't mind coming along, just let me know when you are having a Punjab," said Carl.

Craig laughed.

"Carl, it's not *Punjab*, it is called *Puja*," Nikhil corrected, but couldn't help giggling afterwards. "I'll be happy to come along," said Tom.

"Oh, I don't think my mum and dad will allow me to come, but I'll ask," said Mary, a little uncertain.

Craig said nothing.

"We also celebrate Diwali," continued Nikhil.

"We all know about that," said Craig, gloomily, "we just missed it."

"Are you trying to be funny? We haven't just missed it," remarked Tom. "It's yet to come." Tom hissed between his teeth.

"You can be so pathetic most of the time Craig. I don't find your humour funny, not one bit. My mother told me, at the time of Diwali, we are celebrating victory, of good over evil and light over darkness," said Nikhil.

"That is a good thing," said Craig. "I don't think anyone likes the dark."

"I don't," admitted Mary.

"I don't mind the dark," said Carl.

Nikhil grinned happily. "Me neither Carl," he admitted. "My dad said that Diwali is a time for being friends with everyone and wishing good things to come to others and not just to ourselves, and that is why I am going to ask our Hindu gods and goddesses for help, especially for you Carl," he added proudly.

"That's great, thanks Nikhil," said Carl, with a broad smile.

"What a pity you won't be able to tell us about your god Vishnu," Craig remarked in a sarcastic manner, "Someone's coming, look," he pointed.

Chapter Eleven

A Cry for Help

They all turned and looked down the road.

"It's Trevor!" exclaimed Mary.

"He seems to be in a hurry," suggested Carl.

"He does," agreed Tom.

They all turned in Trevor's direction and hurried towards him.

Craig began to complain again, "We can forget about food I suppose. I am so very hungry." He rubbed his stomach and pulled a face, but his strides got bigger than any of the others. "What's up, Trev?" he shouted.

"My iguana has gone," Trevor yelled back, and he sounded very upset.

They caught up with him.

"What do you mean, your iguana has gone?" asked Craig. "Is he dead?"

"No, no, he's not dead. At least, I don't think so," replied Trevor, looking even more upset because of Craig's thoughtless question.

"Don't you keep him in a cage in your house Trevor?" asked Craig.

"Yeah, but my sister opened the cage door. She left it open and when she returned..."

"Don't tell us, he was gone," Craig remarked, "The flipping lizard must still be somewhere in your house Trevor," he almost barked impatiently.

"No, he is not," replied Trevor, "We looked everywhere." Trevor looked really frustrated.

"He would be difficult to locate so unless he shows his face he'll be hiding in some corner. When he's hungry, like I am, I am sure he will come out and then you can catch him and put him back in its cage, and *feed him*," Craig stressed, "and be more careful next time."

There must be some truth in the saying 'a hungry man is an angry man,' because Craig sounded angry and unsympathetic towards Trevor's plight.

"Don't be so horrible Craig," said Carl. "Trevor, were any of the doors or windows in your house opened?"

"Yes," replied Trevor. "The back door was open. Flip!" Trevor gasped. "It leads to the path that leads to the river." Trevor opened his mouth as if he had suddenly received a shock. "Oh no!" he cried. "He will drown."

Trevor turned and began to run. The others ran after him.

"Don't be silly," cried Carl. "The lizard won't drown."

They caught up with him.

"Lizards are very good swimmers, regardless of their age," said Carl. "There is a stream that flows towards a river not far from my great-grandmother's home in the Caribbean, where I saw lots of baby lizards swimming about in the water."

"In that case, he might just decide to swim off and never return," said Craig.

"Craig, you are being really spiteful! I for one have just about had enough of your unkind remarks," yelled Nikhil. "Can you just listen to yourself?" he asked.

Mary stopped running and began to walk. "I don't know why we are running," she shouted after them. "If the lizard has reached the riverbank, there will be no chance of catching him. He would be in the water by now, so I don't see what good running and letting ourselves become tired and out of breath will do." She bent over and began to rub her chubby thighs and legs and panting.

"I agree," remarked Carl, who also stopped running.

They arrived at the river near Tom's home.

"Well, if the lizard has fallen into this river, you won't see him, not until he crawls out again, six feet tall," Nikhil, who had just told Craig off for being unkind, teased. "Besides, the water is too deep and murky for such a small reptile to be seen," he added.

"Trevor," said Tom, "your house is some distance from mine so what makes you think that the iguana managed to get all the way here?"

"Water from the river flows from here to the back of my house and is quite shallow," replied Trevor.

No sooner had Trevor finished speaking, they noticed his sister, Gaia, hurrying towards them.

"Here she comes," said Trevor, sulkily.

Gaia walked up to them.

"Trev," she said, looking worried. "I am sorry, I really am. I was only trying to help. I thought the lizard would stay in the cage. I only left for a minute. Please don't be mad at me." She blinked and sniffed away a tear. "Anyway, Carl's mum rang. She said that a cat looking like your tabby, Tom, just climbed up the tree in her back garden, at super speed, and is sitting on the very top branch, looking at something." Tom looked a little surprised by Gaia's news.

"I doubt that would be my cat," he said. "Lady H wouldn't know her way here," he told them.

"Yes, she would, Tom," corrected Carl. "The house I live in is your old house," he reminded him.

"Oh, sorry I forgot," said Tom.

"Cats sometimes revisit their old territory," said Carl.

"I think it might be Pinkie up in the tree," suggested Gaia.

"Pinkie, who is Pinkie?" asked Mary with a chuckle.

"We named the iguana Pinkie, because his eyes and tongue seem to go pink at times," Gaia explained timidly.

"Oh, I see," said Mary, a little mystified.

"How odd," admitted Craig.

Nikhil grinned.

"I don't think that cat is Hildegard either Tom," said Gaia. "Carl's mum said it's a small tabby and Lady H is a big cat, isn't she?"

"In that case, it must be a stray," said Tom. "It certainly isn't Clovis. It can't be."

"Yes, I agree. My mum hasn't said we can have him yet, and he's not yet a grown cat, so how would he find his way to my house by himself?"

Carl and Tom looked at each other suspiciously.

"It could be any cat. Tabbies are quite common," Carl added.

"That's right," Tom agreed, "It's not likely that it could be, so there is no need for me to go home and check."

"No, there is no need, and there is no time to waste either," said Carl. "We must go and see whether this cat has gone up the tree in my garden because he has spotted Trevor's Pinkie."

They all giggled before they hastened to Carl's home.

The river was within walking distance of Carl's home, near a place called The Loch. People often sit on the benches nearby, to fish for trout. After each catch, they would throw the fish back into the river, and many people like walking along the path and over the iron bridge, where they would pause to gaze into the water to see whether they might glimpse a fish or two.

The children had walked on quickly past the bridge, with poor Trevor way ahead of them. He looked anxious, and although he didn't voice it, Carl felt sure that he hoped Pinkie was up the tree and not in the river.

After a while, the boys began to run again, and it seemed that they were running as fast as their legs could carry them. Mary and Gaia found it hard to keep up, but eventually they all ran down the gravelled path and dashed through the gate, which led into Carl's back garden.

Carl exclaimed, "I can see the cat Tom, look!" As Tom got closer to him, he spoke for Carl's ears only, "He really does look like Clovis," he said.

It was true. If it wasn't Clovis, it was a look-alike, but they could not see the lizard.

"I don't see Pinkie," said Trevor, looking more nervous than ever.

"He will be difficult to spot," said Carl. "The lizard is nearly the same colour as the leaves and branches of the tree," he reminded.

"Perhaps if we look in the direction where the tabby is facing, we might see what's up there with him," suggested Craig.

As they all turned and looked up towards the top of the tree, they gasped, seeing that a big clump of darkness was swirling around it.

Chapter Twelve

The Crowbates

The dense swirling darkness suddenly became what looked like a big black crow, which continued to circle in the air some distance above the tree. The tabby was keeping watch over something, but the children could not yet see whether it was Trevor's iguana. The kitten did not budge, not even when they thought the crow was about to swoop.

Tom called, "*Clovis*! If it's you up there, please look down."

The young cat didn't even blink.

There followed a big gust of wind in the direction of the tree, and immediately the leafy branches began to sway backwards and forwards, and up and down, quite forcefully, creaking as if at any moment they would snap and fall to the ground. The rustling of the wind could be heard, but not felt by anyone. It was at that moment that once again the area surrounding the tree suddenly grew darker, so dark that they could no longer see it.

Eleanor, who was standing in Carl's bedroom, opened the window and called to them.

"Children," she said, "I don't know what is happening out there, but I think you had all better come on inside. Please leave the lizard and that cat to the mercies of the...."

Eleanor did not finish her statement. Instead, she stood looking surprised because the darkness vanished and the wind died down as suddenly as it had begun. She looked up towards the sky again.

"It looks like rain, the clouds have darkened," she informed them. "I think I had better call the fire brigade right away. They should know what to do about this situation, it is a crisis. I believe that the crow is a bad omen, and is either after the cat or the lizard, but I wouldn't like to guess, which of the two it will attack first. I only hope it doesn't land on this roof. God help us."

Eleanor shook her head before she closed the window and walked away.

"I see him," cried Trevor, pointing upwards. "Look! That flipping crow is about to nosedive at my Pinkie."

The lizard looked as if it was hanging on for dear life.

"Yep," announced Craig, unsympathetically, "It certainly looks as if that crow is about to swoop down and

136

attack or snatch your lizard and carry it off for its dinner. Don't they eat lizards in some countries?" he asked, jokingly.

Mary's left knuckle jabbed into Craig's ribcage.

"*Ouch*! That hurts!" Craig pulled a face at Mary.

"*Good*," she told him rather loudly. "It was meant to. Perhaps now you will stop being such a twerp and be more sensitive towards Trevor's situation."

"Still, you didn't have to be so physical. That hurt!" he yelled again, as if trying to attract attention, rubbing his side and pulling a long face at the same time. "I could have you up for assault. My uncle is a copper!" Pouting and looking miserable, he stepped away from Mary, and stood beside Trevor. No one paid any attention to him.

"We had better do something," suggested Tom.

"What can we do?" asked Nikhil. "Can't you see? I see him clearly now, and that lizard is no baby iguana, like Trevor told us in class. It looks really big and long."

"That's because it has grown," said Gaia, in a rather husky little voice.

"I for one won't be climbing up that tree, even if I could. The branches are no longer strong enough, they look withered. I heard them creaking while the wind was blowing. And even if they *were* strong enough, I don't want to be attacked by that crow," said Nikhil.

"Me neither," grumbled Craig.

Trevor wasn't the only one looking anxious. Gaia and Mary looked worried too.

Eleanor had returned and had reopened the window.

"Carl, Tom, and the rest of you boys and girls, I forbid any of you to attempt to climb that tree," she warned, "It's too dangerous. That crow looks as if it will attack anyone who gets in its way, and those branches really don't look strong enough to hold anyone's weight, I am surprised it is holding the lizard and the cat. Besides, the lizard and the cat are both too far up, not even the extended ladder in the garage would reach them. That is a job for the fire brigade," she counselled.

"We know mum," replied Carl. "Clovis," he called.

This time the kitten turned briefly, and his eyes looked big, round and golden.

"Tom," whispered Carl, "Did you see and did you hear that?"

Tom nodded. The others were too busy fussing over how they might help to get not only the lizard, but also the young cat down, to have seen anything at the time. They would not have heard what was said either because, what was said, was meant for Carl's and Tom's ears only.

Tom moved closer so that only Carl would hear what he had to say.

"Carl, I am sure that tabby is really Clovis." He did not wait for Carl's reply. "I am sure he just said, 'Stop fussing, I will divert the crow and one of you will get the reptile down'."

"Yes," Carl agreed. "I heard that too. But how could it have been the kitten, and how does whoever it was, expect us to get the lizard down? It looks as if it's only us who heard the voice. Are we both losing it, Tom?"

"I know I am not going soft in the head, I heard the voice as clear as I hear you, and I do believe that it was Clovis," said Tom.

Carl, looking astonished, continued in a whisper, "Gosh, Tom, do you, do you really believe that it was Clovis?"

"Yes, I believe because it is not the first time. I have had feelings before that he speaks to me, but now is not the time to tell you about it," said Tom.

"The fire brigade are on their way," Eleanor announced. "But I really can't see how they will reach those two, not even with their longest ladder. Heaven help us," she added, shaking her head, "we certainly need a miracle this afternoon."

Very soon, the fire brigade crew arrived, three men and one woman, and Eleanor was right, not even their longest ladder could reach to where the kitten and the lizard rested.

"From what I can see, there is no way we are going to get that far up," said one of the men. "If we attempt to cut footholds in the trunk of that tree, it might cause a panic and there is no telling what will happen then."

"That crow looks pretty hostile to me," said the woman with them.

"We can't go cutting holes in that tree either," said another of the men, adding, "it's protected."

His three companions looked at him.

"I checked with the Council before we set off," he told them.

"That was good thinking Mullen," said another.

"Trevor," said Craig, "you didn't tell me your dad was a fireman."

Trevor looked even more perturbed. "If my dad can't get to them, no one will." He squirmed as if in discomfort. Noticing, his dad walked over to him and put his arm around his shoulder.

"Don't worry, son. If we can't think of anything to do to help those two creatures, someone else will," he encouraged, looking upwards, his face full of doubts.

"Do you think if we try using the hose, the water will frighten them and cause them to run down the tree?" asked another co-worker. Mullen patted Gaia's shoulder, and she smiled up at her dad before he walked over and re-joined his workmates.

"I don't think that is a good idea," he replied. "Crows like to get at lizards, and I really don't think the water from the hose we have here will reach them, and I have a funny feeling in the pit of my stomach that it wouldn't scare them either, even if it did reach."

The firewoman stood with her mouth wide open, looking up, then she said, "We can't climb it Bill. I won't take the chance with any of you men. That tree is too stout, and there are no grips, even with ropes. Anyway, that creature doesn't look like any crow I have ever seen before," she said.

While the fire-fighters continued to discuss by what means, if any, they might be able to entice the kitten and lizard down from the tree or perhaps scare the crow away, the huge black bird gave out three raucous cries, and in no time, six of the ugliest-looking creatures appeared as if from nowhere. They circled in the air with the crow, which seemed to be growing larger by the minute. As they hovered in the air above, the first crow gave out three more unpleasant cries and another six crows appeared as before.

"That crow must be sending out some kind of message," said Carl.

"I agree. I think he is calling the others to him," said Tom. "Have you noticed, each time he lets out those awful shrieks, six crows appear?"

Tom and Carl were still speaking quietly together.

"No ordinary crow looks like those up there," said Carl.

"You are right again, they are all rather ugly looking, and don't they seem to be growing bigger to you?" asked Tom.

"I think so," Carl replied.

"What is that red patch on the leader? I have never

seen a crow with a red patch before, have you, Carl?" asked Tom.

The two boys had only just finished their conversation, when the same crow gave out another succession of horrendous cries, and for the third time, another six crows materialised.

"That crow works in sixes. Each time it screams, another six appear," said Nikhil.

"That's right, there are eighteen of them up there now," taunted Craig. "How can a little cat and a lizard be shared between so many?"

Trevor looked appalled at Craig's suggestion.

"I agree with you about the big one being the leader Carl," said Tom.

"They are planning something. I dread to guess what that something is," suggested Carl.

"They certainly aren't any fans of mine," said Tom.

"Carl, Tom, you are both right," said Gula, who had arrived and walked up and stood beside them, looking skywards. "They are from the pit of a horrible realm and need to go back there," she informed them.

"I don't care where they have come from or where they should go back to right now," said Trevor, who had overheard what Gula had said. He looked even more distressed. "They are going to eat my Pinkie," he moaned. "My poor pet is done for."

Trevor became even more fretful, but his sorrowful complaints and his pitiful look, earned him no sympathy from Craig.

"Perhaps it's just as well. I wish they would get on with it," he said. "What are you doing keeping such a large reptile as a pet?" he asked scornfully. "It looks like that iguana could be one of those rare ones. I asked my dad about them, the day you announced in class that you were keeping a pet lizard. Not even Mrs Townsend could believe it when you described it, remember? Well, dad showed me pictures of different species of lizards, and from the look of that one up there..." he pointed, "I believe it is in fact one of the type that usually grow up to six feet long. What my father wondered when I described the lizard, was, how the hell did it get into the country. You'll find no lizard like that one in Britain. That's what my dad told me," remarked Craig.

Craig had made his announcement for everyone to hear.

"Wow!" Mary exclaimed.

"He could swallow you whole, Trevor, if that's true," said Gaia, looking troubled.

"Iguanas don't eat flesh, they are vegetarians," said Carl, recalling the information they had been given by their teacher.

"Thank goodness," said Gaia.

"There are crows and there are crows," announced Gula, "but that flock is no good fortune."

The group continued to watch the creatures as they circled around their assumed leader, and as they hovered in the air they recommenced the same shrill sounds.

"They are not pure crows," Gula further informed them. "They are half crow and half bat."

"Which part is the crow and which is the bat?" asked Gaia.

"Sorry, there is no time to explain that now. Take a look and see if you can figure that out for yourself Gaia," replied Gula. "Those up there are called crowbates. The largest of the lot is none other than Mephisto's second-in-command. Another thing, don't be fooled, they are manifestations of Mephisto's Minions."

"*Minions and crowbates*," said Mary, "whatever do you mean?"

Gula ignored her.

"Are they really going to fight over the cat and Trevor's iguana?" asked Gaia, sounding nervous.

"No, I don't think that is the purpose of the gathering. They are not after the lizard, it is just bait. They are after the cat, and that is not a fully grown cat either, it's still a kitten. " replied Gula.

Tom and Carl looked at each other and their eyes widened.

"Why are they after the kitten?" asked Trevor, looking a little less worried.

"Because," replied Gula, "that kitten up there may look like your ordinary everyday tabby, but he is not, and that very large bird-like creature you see up there, is no ordinary bird either. None of them are."

"That is utter rubbish talk and you know it," put in Craig.

Gula looked at him, but said nothing.

"If they are not real birds," said Gaia, "what are they then?"

"Yeah, what are they?" asked Trevor.

"That cat looks like an ordinary tabby cat to me," said Craig.

"And me," agreed Mary.

"Those crows look like ordinary birds to me too, and I like crows," Craig added, with another of his thoughtless grins.

"You would," remarked Nikhil. "As a matter of fact, I see the resemblance," he added, looking at Craig, then up towards the tree.

"I must admit," said Mary, "I can only see crows, a cat, and a lizard."

"That's a kitten up there, not a grown cat. He's... em," Tom coughed. He said no more, remembering what his mother had said to him. He was afraid to say what he really believed in his heart, for fear the others might laugh and think him crazy.

"Boys and girls," called Eleanor, who had stuck her head out of the open window, "whenever you see a bunch like that, all crying together, no one but a wise seer can understand their words."

The creatures, still some distance away, had begun their manoeuvring and squawking once more.

Gula looked up, and then she looked at her brother. "Carl," she said, "why don't you tell the others whose kitten it is up there."

"I think it is Tom's kitten," said Carl.

"I agree," said Tom. "I too believe that the kitten is Clovis."

"You are too friendly with Carl, that's why it's rubbing off," suggested Craig.

"Rubbing off?" questioned Nikhil.

"Yeah," replied Craig, "Tom is becoming as loopy as they are."

"I really don't care what you have to say Craig," Tom replied. "You are just a jealous person."

"He doesn't look any more special than any other cat to me," said Trevor, smirking.

"I don't know why you are suddenly looking so smug, Trevor. Have you stopped fretting over your Pinkie?" asked Nikhil, defensively.

Despite the danger above their heads, some laughed at the mention of Trevor's pet's name.

"It *is* him, it's Clovis up there," Carl admitted, with a serious expression on his face.

"I think the kitten is guarding the lizard from the crows," suggested Nikhil.

"I do too," agreed Gaia, bravely.

"The kitten's purpose is not only to guard the

lizard," said Gula. "Their leader is a subordinate of Mephisto. His second in command, and one of the angels, cast out of heaven."

"Yes," said Carl, "and Mephisto knows who the kitten really is and why he has come, so he is using the lizard, in the hope that he and his minions will get to destroy him or that he might fall to his death, from such a great height."

Most of the youngsters listening to Gula's story, looked baffled.

"That won't happen, they won't destroy Clovis," said Tom.

"No, they can't, but that won't stop them from trying," said Carl.

"Don't be so ridiculous," said Craig, raising his voice. "Are you expecting the rest of us to believe that the tabby cat, is not really a cat, and that those creatures are not really crows? Who might Trevor's Pinkie be?" he asked mockingly.

"You can tease all you like Craig," said Carl. "The problem with you is, you have a very limited imagination for someone who has such a way with words."

"And you, Carl, and your best pal, Tom here, and

your wacky sister, are talking gibberish," responded Craig, and then he pulled a face. "Crows like to attack lizards, and that is just what they are after, Trevor's Pinkie," he concluded, sticking out his neck at them.

"*No!*" cried Trevor.

"Yes, and if the cat gets in their way, they will no doubt take care of him too - Incidentally, I don't believe that's a kitten up there. It might look small, but I believe it's a grown cat," cried Craig. "There's no way, Clovis, would be able to find his way here without getting lost, and even if he did, and I'm being hypothetical, there's no way he would be able to climb that tree."

"Yeah," agreed Trevor.

"Whose side are you on Trevor?" asked Nikhil. "I think we should stop criticising and arguing, and think about what can be done for the lizard and the kitten, especially you, Trevor. It would really wipe the smile off your face if one of those crows or whatever they are up there, snatched your pet."

Trevor's face lost its colour, and he wasn't smiling anymore either.

"All it takes is one swoop and one gulp," continued Nikhil, deliberately, "and your precious Pinkie will become crowbates indigestion." Nikhil wasn't smiling. Trevor face went quite pale, and he looked horrified. He swallowed heavily as the crowbates lined up and commenced their hideous squawks yet again.

Chapter Thirteen

The Shadow

"I suppose you are the seer here Gula," suggested Craig. "You seem to understand what they are squawking about."

Gula knew Craig was mocking her so she did not answer him. Instead, she closed her eyes and cocked her head to one side, as if listening to someone or something. After a while, she opened her eyes and straightened up. As Gula spoke, she became surrounded by what looked like golden rays, which only Carl and Tom seemed able to see. It was coming from the long mark at the back of her leg, just above her ankle. They had already experienced a similar happening in the past, so they knew what Gula was capable of.

"Those creatures," said Gula.

"Crows," interrupted Craig.

Gula ignored Craig.

"They resemble diurnal birds of prey," she informed them.

Craig looked puzzled.

"'I mean birds that are active during the daytime.'" she continued, "birds that have 'broad wings, a short hooked bill and strong talons.'"

Craig stared at Gula.

"I mean hooked claws. And they also have long tails. Those you see up there-" she pointed and looked towards the sky, "they are what Mephisto have turned some of his followers into. As I mentioned before, they are crowbates."

Most of the children gasped and immediately looked fearful.

"Good heavens," said Eleanor, who now stood nearby watching and listening. "Children, you had all better come inside right this minute. Hurry up now," she ordered, with a look of concern on her face as she walked away and headed for the kitchen door. "By the sound of it, there might not be anything left to rescue," she told them, to Trevor's renewed dismay.

The others moved closer to Gula, and she continued as though she hadn't heard her mother's advice. They all seemed keen to hear more of her explanation. This time Gula did not tilt her head and she did not close her eyes, but she was still surrounded by the golden rays.

"They have all taken the form of bird-bats because Mephisto wasn't able to change them into simple crows. They believe they will be able to foil the plans of the higher heavenly ones."

"That is how ambitious Mephisto has always been," Carl added, which surprised his friends, but not his sister.

"Well, if what you say is true," remarked Craig, "not that I believe you for a minute, it is written, the devil did fool Eve."

"Who said?" barked Trevor.

"I do, I say." Craig retaliated harshly.

"Yes," replied Gula, "you are right about that, Craig. And before our mission is accomplished, he will fool many more. He has already fooled one of us, who has now become a strong influence to a few others."

Craig suddenly recalled the small bottle he had been given by the strange man, and how well he sang and still sings. A queer feeling came over him. But then, as if he had second thoughts, he grinned dismissively. He watched defiantly as they all looked around at each other, even the fire-fighters.

Tom suddenly remembered how Clovis had begun

to wink at him before he left home, but he had taken no notice. Now he understood the reasons for the winks. But Craig and Trevor looked as though they had decided that their friend Carl, had a crazy sister, who liked to make up frightful stories. They didn't have the nerve to voice their opinion at that moment, but despite what they thought, it was evident that they were all captivated by her.

"Like I said earlier," continued Gula, "Mephisto is another name for a being some people call the devil. In Spanish, he is called Diablo...."

"She is right," interrupted Eleanor. "He was once an angel of mighty stature until he became rebellious and refused a direct order from the godhead, the Great Elohim."

Gula looked at her mother and smiled.

"This once-angelic being had the most beautiful voice anywhere in the heavenly realms," said Gula.

On hearing that new bit of information, Craig's face changed colour and the nauseating feeling took hold of him once more.

Most of the children looked on and listened. They were becoming more and more intrigued by the story Gula was relating so that, for a while, they appeared to have lost all recollection of what was happening, or what was about to take place in the air, over their very heads.

"I am not crazy, I am speaking facts not fiction," said Gula, looking directly at Craig. "Clovis is not in the safety of Tom's home," she continued, her voice growing louder as she spoke.

"What?" Craig exclaimed. "Now I have heard everything! Are you kidding?" He looked unimpressed and so did Trevor, and even Luke, who had walked out from among the crowd and stood beside Craig. They had seen the kitten so they felt that Gula had gone a little too far and was simply making up stories. Nikhil, however, did not share their views. He glanced up towards Clovis, and then he looked at Gula and smiled. Gula smiled back.

"It was Mephisto who frightened my mum, years ago, before I was born..." she further informed them.

Gula paused again, as if to listen once more.

"I knew it! What have I been saying all these years?" Eleanor joined in, "Children, listen to what my Gula has to say, she is not crazy," was her firm advice.

Gula cocked her head to one side once more and, as before, after a little while, she straightened up again. This time, as she began to speak, the rays around her were no longer golden, but purple and gold. They became stronger and more pronounced, now visible for all to see, causing many to step away from her, with mixed reactions.

"If she is not crazy, she is certainly a little witch," said one of the neighbours, who were standing in the next garden watching.

"And that means the mother must be a bigger one," commented a man who had climbed over the partition wall two doors away.

A woman standing beside him grumbled and nodded her agreement.

While Gula spoke, the crowbates slowly began to descend, and as they drew closer, it was evident that they had all continued to grow larger, and the one everyone assumed was the leader, looked gigantic. After a while, they hovered in the air again ceremoniously, and as before, they bunched up together and recommenced their screeching. The tabby remained still and focused.

"Why won't the cat come down from the tree? I am sure he could if he wanted to," remarked Mary.

"What about Pinkie?" asked Gaia.

"That's right, what about the lizard," said Nikhil. "Is it to be left on its own up there?"

No one replied.

Gula continued her story. "It was Mephisto who was eventually cast out of heaven, but it wasn't straight after he'd attempted to defy the High One. He had pretended to show remorse, and many took pity on him at the time and so he was granted a reprieve. He certainly fooled some because they had failed to report it to the high council of elders."

While Gula continued speaking, she kept vigilant. "But the Great One didn't need to be told," she went on. "Being the highest Elohim, he knew that Mephisto, who at the time was as beautiful and as radiant as a morning star, had spent time during the postponement, making himself look even prettier and singing even more beautifully."

Once again, Craig remembered the strange man, and how everyone had marvelled at his sudden ability to sing so well. He had even made the front page in the local newspaper. "They couldn't be talking about the same person," he muttered to himself.

Carl looked as though he was in a daze before he began to speak.

"Mephisto also led the choir too in the highest heavenly realms, whilst secretly gathering up his army of followers. They were made up of rebellious angels whose hearts and minds he had managed to corrupt. The mortals who follow him are those he charmed with false promises." Carl raised his voice and pointed towards the sky. "That is not him up there," he cried. "But he is definitely coming for sure!"

Gula looked at her brother briefly and then she looked at Craig.

"Man!" cried Craig, clearly irritated by them, "I have heard enough of this hogwash. These two are just time-wasting storytellers."

Craig walked away and sat on the step by the back door of the house and immediately he began to shiver.

"Someone ought to call an ambulance for this one," remarked a strange-looking teenage girl who suddenly appeared in the garden. No one saw her enter because the gate was closed and one of the fire-brigade men was leaning on it. The garden walls and even the hedges were too high for her to have climbed over. At her suggestion, some looked towards Craig.

"I don't mean the tormented one, I meant *this* one." She pointed at Gula.

Gula said nothing. She did not even look at the girl,

but Tom, Carl and Nikhil, gave her a disapproving look.

The crowbates had bunched up even closer together once more, but this time their movements and sounds appeared as if they might be having some kind of disagreement.

"Then Mephisto did the dumbest thing," continued Gula, ignoring the girl, who looked just about her own fourteen years, but not as tall. "He confronted the Highest Elohim."

"He's an Idiot," remarked Nikhil, in a quiet voice.

"So he is," agreed Gula.

"The girl is right. That is when he was thrown out of the kingdom," said a tall slim elegant looking woman, who had walked up and stood beside Carl. She had short flaming red hair and her pretty face looked unusually bright. She wore a long black and gold dress, and a half-length loosely fitted jacket and ankle-length boots. "Mephisto wasn't cast down to this earth. He and his followers were banished into an outer realm. Much later on, somehow, he found his way up to this earth, bringing his minions and devilish ways with him," she said.

The woman looked scornfully at the creatures in the air, before she continued her explanation. "It was while

Mephisto, and those you see up there, were on their way down from the heavenly realm that they lost all their capacity for good, and the light they once carried turned to darkness. They lost their spiritual bodies, and became flesh and blood, but Mephisto, now the master of all evil, knows how to manipulate them. He knows how to bend them to his will. He can change then into whatever shape or form he desires." The woman paused and looked at Carl. "Another thing this young boy is right about - Mephisto is not up there, not yet, but he is coming, for certain. Don't underestimate him, he can turn those followers of his into demonic spirits. If you become possessed by one of those, you will begin to behave intensely frantic and even wild at times."

"Yeah, disbelieving and negative too," put in Carl.

Tom looked at his friend and then at Craig. Craig remained silent now with his mouth gaping, as he stared from Gula to Carl, and then at the woman.

"Very few mortals, beasts of the fields and fowls of the air are safe from these tormentors and beguilers. Only the chosen ones and those who come from a place of love and are pure in heart can ever detect and defeat Mephisto and his followers," continued the woman, who was the second stranger to have appeared in the garden.

She looked from Carl to Gula, then at Tom, Mary, Gaia and Nikhil.

"That beguiler Mephisto, knows that the end for them is coming, so he will try all he can to prevent it, but he and his followers must be cast down before the happening," she said.

Craig laughed hilariously and so did Trevor, Luke and several others.

"The *happening*?" asked Craig from where he sat, with a look of total disbelief.

The lady ignored Craig, but he persisted.

"And who are you?" he asked.

"My name is Huldah. I am a prophetess of this time. I was sent to bear witness to this day's events."

Craig, disbelieving, laughed comically, and so did quite a few others. The woman, ignoring their cynicism turned to face Carl, she said, "Carl, the egg, given to you by one from above. Please go and get it and be quick about it."

"How does she know about the egg?" asked Tom.

Carl looked at his sister. They should have been surprised, but neither of them looked it, and neither of them spoke either. Instead, Carl headed for the house and had to push Craig out of the way as he was sat on the floor, blocking the entrance to the door. Carl ran inside the house. In no time at all he returned carrying a large golden egg. It was so large that everyone marvelled, wondering how he managed to carry it without help.

"Here," said Carl, stretching his hands containing the large oval-shaped golden egg towards Huldah.

Craig had stood up and was leaning against the wall, and like the other bystanders, he too looked curiously amazed at the size of this golden egg.

The woman looked at Gula. "*Now*, Gula," she said, "we don't have much time, the Shadow is nearby."

"Put the egg on the ground before me," said Gula.

Carl did as he was told, and the others stood anxiously waiting, their eyes staring at the spot where Carl had gently placed the egg.

"That's the egg you found Carl, in your back garden, months ago - I didn't realise it was so massive, wow!" said Nikhil.

More people who lived nearby heard the children's voices and the commotion and had come out of their houses and into their gardens, watching and wondering what was taking place. Some were looking out from their upstairs windows. "Here, what's all the commotion?" asked an old man, squinting and struggling to put on his glasses. He tried to climb over the green hedge that separated his garden from another nearby, but got stuck. Gula noticed, raised her hands into the air and immediately the man was lifted up and moved as light as a feather into their garden.

"Here...em...here, what are you up to?" the old man asked looking petrified, as Gula moved him with her hands as if by magic, and placed him to stand beside her. "Please be quiet now old man," said Huldah, the woman who had introduced herself as a prophetess.

Gula stooped down beside the egg and touched it seven times, muttering words that were clearly not English. The golden egg began to move about slowly, and then it began to spin around and around, faster and faster, like a spinning top.

Gula then stood up and spread her arms outwards and then she pointed them upwards towards the sky. The sleeves of the top she was wearing appeared as if they were wings.

"She looks like an angel," marvelled Gaia, to Mary, in a soft voice.

Mary whispered back to Gaia.

"She does, my goodness, she does," she said, looking amazed.

Gula spoke words aloud, which no one understood.

"Comma-nomatenda-EleEle-elme-rati-enda-moso-commo-ota-emadata-attaka." (Come forth now, Eagle People, from the star realms sent, attack.)"

While Gula spoke in this strange unknown language, her whole body had risen up, and she was surrounded by a marvellous golden light, which emanated from the long mark at the back of her ankle. She was lifted off the ground and was floating above them all. She was radiant, bathed in the most glorious beam of light imaginable. She then descended, brought back down to the earth by nothing visible, to the others who watched in awe. As Gula finished speaking, to the utter astonishment of everyone standing in the back garden that Saturday afternoon, the golden egg opened and seven golden eagles flew out and up into the sky.

They raced towards the eighteen crowbates, and as they flew upwards they grew larger and larger, even larger than the crowbates and their leader, larger than any bird ever seen by human eyes, in this or any other recorded lifetime. The eagles flew swiftly up into the air where a battle commenced. Gasps and cries could be heard in the garden that day, as the eagles clashed with crowbates, and different-coloured sparks began to fly about in the sky. Then, some distance away, out of what looked like a thick grey mass of fog, there appeared a large shadowy-type creature with a large fork-like instrument in its hand, blazing as if it had just been dipped in a fiery furnace.

Chapter Fourteen

The Burning Bush

The prophetess Huldah, began to speak hurriedly. "Carl," she said, "the goddess awaits It is time, you know what to do, go now."

Gula waved both hands as if to hurry her brother along, but suddenly, in a flash, he was way beyond the huge tree at the very end of their garden.

"What is it? Time for what?" asked Craig, facing Gula, who had used magic to place her brother where he now stood, before a row of bushs, muttering to himself.

"Gula," said Craig, "I hope you are not crazy enough to allow your brother to attempt anything. My mum used to read me stories about people like you. You two are much too young to be practising witchcraft and wizardry. What you are allowing this strange nutter to force your brother to do is insane, madness. He'll not make it! Do you know this woman?" he asked loudly, pointing at Huldah. "Do you know who she really is?" he cried.

"Be silent for once boy!" a voice ordered.

Everyone looked around. Some turned towards the strange girl questioningly, thinking that it might have been her, since the voice was that of a female.

The young girl shook her head. "Don't look at me," she said.

Craig blushed, bit his lip and said no more.

Carl felt the urgency of the moment. He felt something stirring inside him. He didn't know what it was, but he wasn't afraid. He remembered the time before, when he was compelled to walk into the burning bush, and the fire did not harm him. There was a tabby cat in the fire, wearing a golden diadem on its head. It was the same woman's voice, which had spoken to him back then. He remembered she had told him certain things, especially the part when she said that if he ever needed her help in the future, he was not to hesitate, but to call on her. He wondered whether he would see her this time, and not just hear her voice.

The people in the back garden, were all watching with bated breath, wondering why Carl, stood in front of the bush, ignoring what was taking place in the air.

Carl whispered, but his voice was not soft enough, they all heard him.

"Bast," he said.

They looked at each other, dumbfounded, wondering why Carl was standing there muttering the word, 'Bast' to himself.

"What on earth is Carl up to?" asked Trevor, with an idiotic grin on his face. "I really don't know who is weirder, Carl or his sister."

"Perhaps the whole family are a little loco," Luke replied. "You heard their mother earlier."

"What have I been trying to tell all of you, he's clearly gone bananas, he's talking to himself," suggested Craig.

"How can you say those things Luke, Trevor, and you Craig?" asked Nikhil. "After what you are witnessing here today, plus all you have heard." He looked at Craig, "You and your pals are the ones who are nuts."

They continued watching and heard when Carl called out again, but this time he spoke much louder, and he called, "*Bastet*!" instead of Bast.

All went quiet and everyone was very still as a cool breeze began to blow, and at that very moment, to their profound amazement, the bush Carl stood before began to blaze, and in the centre was the faint outline of a tall person with the head of a cat and the body of a human being. Only Carl saw her. Frightened, Gaia cried out.

"*Trevor, hurry, please hurry*! Get the hose and turn it on quickly. Carl is on fire, he's set himself alight!"

Trevor, in his fearful misguided state, dashed for the hose, which was already attached to the water pipe on the wall of the house. They had used it on several occasions, in their summer water fights with Carl and their other friends. Trevor turned the tap on and ran towards the burning bush, but dropped the hose and took several paces backwards, looking startled. They all heard the voice commanding Carl.

"Enter Carl," said the female-sounding voice.

Mary and Gaia, finding some comfort in holding hands, looked shocked. Many gasped again, but Tom didn't because he recognised the voice. It was as clear as the evening when they sat in the living room at home, the evening Gula gave healing to Clovis, and afterwards he, Carl and Gula, had heard the same voice. She had said many things, but had specifically mentioned Clovis.

Everyone watched as Carl walked into the burning bush, he did not hesitate.

Craig looked horrified now. A few began to shake in fear when suddenly, to their further astonishment, Carl was no longer visible to them.

"That was quick, cinders, he is burned up, he has gone," whispered Trevor, looking flabbergasted.

"Oh dear," said Mary, "poor Carl." She became tearful.

Gaia, who had begun to cry, put her hands to her face to try and conceal her tears. "Carl set the place and himself alight," she murmured mournfully.

The others remained in a state of shock.

"He will be back," Gula assured them in a calm voice. But the majority did not believe her.

"I have seen that glowing bush somewhere before. Do not be afraid," said Eleanor from where she stood. "I think it was in a vision. A little heavenly glory has come down to earth. We are truly blessed. Carl has not been burnt to ashes; he is about his heavenly mother's and father's business. You heard Gula, her brother will be back."

Luke, as if awakened by Eleanor's words, looked towards her, and finding his voices once more, he shook his head pitifully and stuttered a little at first, "They are real fruitcakes this family. They really believe that Carl will be back." He continued shaking his head. "I can't believe what has happened just now. Is it real? All we came into this garden for, was to try and get your Pinkie, Trevor." Trevor, looking quite ill, took a little time to respond. When he did, he sounded feeble.

"I wonder what Carl's dad is like?"

"I have met Phillip," said Craig.

Trevor and Luke looked at Craig, expectantly.

"Oh, he seems a well-adjusted bloke."

Trevor shook his head as they turned to gaze at the fiery bush once more. The water from the hose was flooding the area beyond the tree where the bush continued to glow. Gula raised her hands and pointed towards the area, and immediately the water soaked away into the earth, and the hose recoiled itself back in its rightful place, next to the pipe on the wall.

Suddenly, the firewoman cried out. "What's happening now?" She pointed towards the tree top. Everyone turned and looked towards the pinnacle of the tree where the tabby cat had been sitting, and saw a bright light shining on that area. To the great astonishment of the people, the kitten was no longer there, but in his place sat an enormous golden lion, his eyes fixed on the shadowy creature.

Still looking up, Eleanor shouted, "That lion is not of this world! Are my eyes deceiving me, what's that other creature up there? This is just too much in one day. Am I really seeing what I'm looking at? That ugly creature looks like the ghoulish fiend that chased me years ago, when I was pregnant with Gula!"

"Good, Mephisto has arrived!" yelled the strange-looking girl.

"Is that its name?" asked Gaia, who still looked petrified.

"Yes, one of our Master's many names," replied the girl brightly.

"Unless the creature is forced to transform, it will be hard to suppress him," said Huldah, with a frown.

The lion stretched out its two front paws and roared. Suddenly, lightning flashed across the sky and like a mighty whip, lashed out towards the crowbates.

A lasso of electrical charge scattered them, separating the leader from the pack. And what was even more astonishing, the whole tree became silver and gold in colour and its branches looked stout and strong.

The shadowy creature attacked the lion with the long forked instrument. It pierced the lion's side, causing him to bleed.

Mary cried out, "Jesus, Mary and Joseph, It looks like the lion took a hit!"

"Good. One up for you my master, Shody," taunted the young stranger, then laughed, and her laughter was not the sort one would normally hear from a teenager, it was the kind of cackle you would expect to come from an evil witch.

"She's just called the Shadow, Shody," said Nikhil.

"So she did, and the name is most befitting, it suits him," replied Huldah. Nikhil looked a little confused.

"He's nothing but crap, really. Think about it. Would you allow him to be anything else, to you?"

Nikhil, surprised now by Huldah's bold loose term for the Shadowy creature, simply shook his head.

"Don't look so astonished. That wench, she did say he's known by many names. Shody must be what he's also called, when he assumes the shape of the Shadow, and Shody, means nothing but crap, to me at any rate," she said.

Two mighty roars came out of the lion's mouth, resounding like thunder, as he manoeuvred in the air. Instantly the blood stopped gushing from the lion's side and the wound was instantly healed. The miraculous thing was, not one drop of the blood from the great lion fell onto the ground, but dissolved in the air. The fiend gave out a gruesome cry, which echoed all around, as it struck out at the lion again.

The lion moved more swiftly this time and let out a third roar and the tree shook as he leaped into the air to meet the Shadow. The lion's whole body lit up instantly with a radiant glow. While more fire gushed from the Shadow's fork, it was dodged and met by water from the lion's mouth.

The Shadow began to change, and in no time became a huge fiery winged red dragon. The dragon was larger than the crowbates and the eagles.

"Good, Lord Drago, the devourer!" cried the teenager, becoming even more excited at the scene. "Now that lion's roast meat, keep watching, there'll be plenty to go round for you carnivorous humans," shouted the malevolent-looking youngster, clearly on the side of the evil one. She laughed idiotically and pointed towards the sky. All watched in terror as the dragon tore across the sky.

"Drago? Oh crikey! Mephisto has turned himself into a dragon," said Nikhil, looking terrified. "He has a name for every form he takes."

Huldah, nodded her head and then she said, "I'm glad you didn't call him Lord. His dragon form is one of his most ruthless, he consumes his victims by flames, and he's a beast not a Lord." Nikhil, looking even more horrified, turned his head once more and followed Hulda's gaze towards the sky.

In a flash, the terrible-looking red dragon circled and raced towards the great lion, lashing out fiercely in all directions with its enormous long thick tail; spitting fire and brimstones from its enormous fanged mouth, his long throat a tunnel of flaming fire.

Some distance away in the air, the golden eagles still battled with the crowbats. Two of the eagles got hit by a black substance that flew out of the crowbates' mouths. This appeared to have rendered the eagles weak because they began to fall from the sky, as the crowbats clawed ferociously, spitting more and more of the dark gunk at them. Golden rays had formed around the other eagles, which prevented them from coming to any harm.

One of the unharmed eagles released a clear substance from its mouth, which, when it touched a crowbate became a silver cord, which magically wound itself around it and immobilised the birdlike creature. A thick dark green shield surrounded the remaining crowbates, and they transformed into humanoids with flames of fire blazing from their hands and horned heads. The eagles immediately transformed themselves too, and became giant golden angelic beings, surrounded by purple rays, and a silver sceptre appeared in each of their hands, and the fight intensified.

One of the golden beings, realising what had happened, dashed after the two falling eagles and waved his sceptre. The falling eagles stopped falling and were instantly enveloped in a radiant glow of light, and immediately they too were transformed into powerful-looking angelic beings and shielded by a forcefield of golden rays. The seven together again, advanced towards the evil humanoids, waving their sceptres at them, each sceptre emitting what looked like powerful streaks of light. From the ground, all looked up at the war raging between the angelic beings and the demonic looking humanoids, just beneath the clouds above.

The lion stretched out in the air, ready to meet the boulder flame-spitting red dragon, but as he turned his head, he was caught off guard. The dragon opened its mouth and fired a great fiery boulder at the lion, which knocked him and sent him flying towards the clouds in the sky. The clouds parted and the lion opened his mouth and sucked the fiery boulder into it with his breath and swallowed it.

The dragon spat many boulders at super speed towards the lion, which was sat on a big thick cloud. The lion blew a ferocious wind from his mouth, which sent the fiery boulders back to its owner, knocking him about in the air. He then gave out a mighty roar, which shook even the clouds above and the earth's surface so that everything and everyone nearby shuddered and cried out in alarm, as parts of the ground nearby were ripped apart immediately it was hit by the sudden quake.

People dodged and rushed away from the cracks, which created deep holes in the ground, for fear they might fall into them. Many panicked and cried out in terror, when they saw grotesque malevolent gargoyle looking female and male creatures, called Gogs and Magogs, begin to appear up through the opening cracks.

The children and people watching the battle became frantic and ran towards the door of the house screaming, when a Gog grabbed a woman and swallowed her whole. Gula, realising what had happened, waved her hands swiftly, at the same time speaking aloud, more unearthly language, "Comatao-noea-denaiele-sepata-comato-sheldatatos." (Come out shield of DenaiEle, separate evil from good, protect.)

This briefly suppressed the creatures. She then stretched her hand behind her back and immediately a massive amount of purple rays appeared from the long mark she was born with, just above her ankle. It formed a shield around the house, across the doorway and around everyone except the strange young woman, who grimaced as if in pain and shifted away quickly from Gula. She must have been invisible to the underground creatures or protected from them because, they took no notice of her, and instead, they began to grapple at the protective shield, which surrounded the onlookers.

Still able to see the action, the petrified crowd witnessed another great astonishment, when a large golden eagle with rainbow markings burst through the clouds. The eagle circled the sky beyond the fighting, and

179

then flew towards the pinnacle of the tree.

"Look at that eagle!" exclaimed Nikhil.

"What a spectacular bird," one of the firemen exclaimed.

"Where did it come from?" another asked, as they looked towards the sky.

"Prehistoric," said a man nearby. A woman next to him began to tremble and cry. Gula noticing, touched the shield which protected her from harm, and immediately the woman stopped crying and was steady on her feet.

"Look!" cried Tom, "the eagle is becoming larger."

Great flashes of different-coloured sparks of light exploded like fireworks and covered the sky, as the eagle spread its wings and flapped them fiercely towards the tree. The tree instantly became the green leafy tree once more, but with sturdy branches.

Meanwhile the Gogs and Magogs, continued their frenzied attack on the shield, uttering strange words and sounds, as they fought furiously to get at the people. Then a powerful looking Gog, stepped forward and cried out in rage, "Sldatididi!" He had motioned with his whole body. This must have weakened one section of the forcefield because, the instant he spoke the word, a hole appeared and a man fell forwards and was grabbed and immediately swallowed whole by one of the female Magogs.

By the time Gula realised what had happened, there was nothing she could have done at that late stage to save the man. She looked sorrowful, as she saw the man's last shoe being devoured. She waved her hands swiftly. "How could I have missed," she whispered, shaking her head in disappointment. Then she cried out in a loud angry voice, "Impitrata-thikata," (Impenetrable, thicker,) and immediately the tear in the shield was sealed once more and the forcefield looked much stronger than when it first appeared around the people. Unable to break through the protective shield again, and looking furious because he was deprived of his capture, the horrible male Gog, turned on the female Magog, and they began to fight each other, until the largest of the Magogs, who must have been their leader, spoke a strange word, and immediately, Gogs and Magogs formed a line. They looked ready for a brutal attack.

The giant eagle flew down towards the unwelcome visitors, circled and spewed a thick white substance from its mouth. As the liquid caught the creature, some of them were badly burnt, and a few were burnt to ashes. The remaining Gogs and Magogs, ran uttering many fiendish cries, as they retreated back down into the cracks in the ground. Wailing was heard as gusts of the thick substance from the eagle's mouth, cascaded down into the large openings, before the cracks closed, sealing up the ground once more.

"Do you think a portal has been opened?" said Nikhil.

"I do hope not," said Huldah. "If that happens, there is no telling what might happen one day, now that those creatures have found a way up," she added, looking concerned.

"Fear not, you two," said the eagle from above, "That portal is now sealed, it cannot be reopened." The crowd gazed skywards in astonishment when they heard the eagle spoke.

Chapter Fifteen

Mephisto

While the battle continued, the dragon transformed into humanoid form and became a great, tall beastly looking creature. Someone in the crowd cried out.

"Oh my God help us. Look at that great beast of a man!"

"That's Mephisto!" cried Gula.

"Yes, His Majesty!" cried the teenage visitor, who curtseyed and bowed at the same time.

Instantly, the hideous-looking creature began to direct boulders of fire from its huge mouth and hands, while propelling fire from his eyes and the top of its rather large elongated head. Mephisto had caused even the fire he was emitting, to roll into many more fiery boulders, which he directed at the lion.

The lion received many horrific blows, and was eventually knocked once more behind the clouds. Mephisto's boulders, which he hurled towards the cloud, grew larger and larger as the cloud parted. Unharmed, the lion stood firmly on what looked like a large clump of blue cloud, and large pools of water gushed from his mouth. The water quenched the fire and the boulders immediately dissolved. None of the boulders, water, or the fire, fell to the earth, they simply evaporated into thin air. Then the lion gave out a mighty roar, and the cloud closed up once more.

With the lion gone, the giant eagle instantly transformed into a tall young man dressed in the colours of the rainbow. He looked at Mephisto, crossed his hands and raised them towards the sky, "It's been a long time coming Mephisto," he said for all to hear, "but I promise you, a change is coming."

"For who, me or you?" cried Mephisto, "Who are you to order change? Here on this planet, change will come, but from me," he boasted vigorously.

The sight of Mephisto, and the sound of his voice caused everyone to shake with fear, but the young man smiled, "I see you don't remember me, as you no longer remember yourself." The beastly looking humanoid laughed.

"And who are you, pray tell," he mimicked with a half bow, while being vigilant.

The young man replied, "I am as you were, yet far

greater then you. I am that I am who sent me. I am the Morning Star, the first and the last. I was sent to help stop you and to cast you down where you belong, into the pit that has been specially designed for you and your kind."

Mephisto laughed again mockingly, "You, a mere boy, and the alpha and omega."

"No, Mephisto. I have come from the Omnipotence."

Mephisto held his head upwards and cried, "The all-powerfulness!" He laughed idiotically. So great was his laughter that the clouds above shook.

"Yes, believe it," said the young man. "I am called by many names. For this mission, I am Rainbow Morning Star. Now speak my name and shudder in your ugly boots," said the young man boldly.

In defiance, Mephisto spoke the name, Morning Star, and attempted to laugh again, but could not because he began to tremble in his boots and all over his body and could not stop. The young man laughed.

"Now call the name Rainbow Morning Star, and you may stop shaking," commanded the young man in amusement. Mephisto did as he was advised to do, and immediately the trembling left him.

"It is time for you to stop your destructive works on this earth and its people."

Mephisto's demonic voice echoed, "Never!"

The young man then spoke words, which no mortal human would understand, "Etaeta dentende immata whipata." (Begotten not made, come rodwhip.)

He raised his hands and pulled them down towards his chest. Immediately, a long rainbow-coloured rod appeared before him, and as he held it, the bottom half of the rod turned into a whip, emitting what appeared to be flashing lightning.

"I told you when we meet again that I would give you the beating of your life. I can tell you don't remember that either," he said.

Mephisto barked, "I remember all I need to remember. I am prince of this world. You, whip me? Never! I will be the ruler of this earth plane or I will destroy it and all that dwells upon it!" He screamed. Then he let out a great big laughter, which echoed all around, but his laughter quickly subsided as the first blow from the young man's lightening flashing rainbow coloured rodwhip reached him. Mephisto acted quickly after the first blow. He grabbed the end of the whip as it was being pulled back, and even though he howled and grimaced because his hands were being scorched, he still held on to it and hurled it with Rainbow Morning Star, still holding onto it, away from him, far up in the air so that the young man and his rodwhip, touched the clouds.

"You and I boy, we are so much alike in one aspect, neither of us will show mercy. Accept this fact seedling, you are no match for the mighty Mephisto." He pounded his chest boastfully. "You are nothing but a sapling weasel. You cannot beat me and you will never be able to suppress me and you know it," he cried aloud, and then he let out a succession of idiotic laughter once more.

In a flash Rainbow Morning Star was facing Mephisto once more, and he spoke again in a heavenly language, "Powata ot mayama medata miemi shielata comatomie." (The power of my mother created me my shield, come to me.) Immediately a rainbow coloured shield appeared around him and a helmet of the same colours covered his head.

As soon as the shield and helmet appeared around Rainbow Morning Star, his rodwhip began to strike out, but Mephisto began to skip and jump and manoeuvred himself away. He managed to dodge most of the blows from the mighty rodwhip, until Rainbow Morning Star cried, "Speedata betata."(Speed away beat away.)

Mephisto could no longer skip nor jump away from the beating. No matter where he placed himself with his evil magic, the rodwhip in the young man's hand was lashing out at him, rainbow coloured lightening flashes. Mephisto began to howl and grimace from the agony of it all so that two great horns protruded from his ears, two from his crown, two from his forehead, and one pushed its way up at the back of his enormous head.

Tom cried out, "Great balls of fire! Mephisto has seven horns."

"I see them. He is getting a taste of his own medicine," said Gula, and she and Huldah, laughed happily.

Fire gushed through Mephisto's horns towards Rainbow Morning Star, and seven golden diadems, adorned with many priceless Jewells, which he stole from the heavenly keep just before he was banished, flew from the horns and hovered in the air above him. In the meantime, the seven eagles who had transformed into angelic beings, had managed to trap Mephisto's minions, into a red forcefield, which they were franticly pushing against, but was unable to free themselves. As Rainbow

Morning Star, gazed at the diadems, Mephisto seized the opportunity, and with his evil magic and his strength, he quickly snatched the rodwhip from the young man's hand, raised it and struck the young man several times, with his own instrument, but not one blow penetrated the shield, which was formed around Rainbow Morning Star, because the shield and helmet was impossible to penetrate.

The young man then spoke again in what must have been words of power, because immediately, the rodwhip fell from Mephisto's hand. Mephisto tried to use his evil magic words once more, to retrieve the rodwhip, but instead, the rodwhip manoeuvred in the air as if it was doing a dance. The rainbow-clad young man shouted words, which this time everyone understood, "Rodwhip, dissolve away." The rodwhip turned into a solid rod, before it dissolved in the air for all to see.

The seven angelic beings joined Rainbow Morning Star, and together they overpowered Mephisto and used their angelic powers combined, to transport the evil one into the red forcefield. Once caged with his minions, Mephisto stretched out his two large thick hairy claw fingered hands, and made a sign, and instantly all his horns began to blaze again. Using more evil magic, he succeeded in placing the young man above the shield and began to pull him towards his flaming horns. With only a few inches left before the blazing horns would pierce him, the seven angelic beings raised their hands and pointed their sceptres. They opened their mouths to speak, but the young man cried out, once again in words everyone understood.

"Stand aside and see the power from the Great Elohim who sent me." The young man crossed his arms swiftly towards the sky and then at Mephisto, and an endless succession of lightning showered from the young man's hands, striking Mephisto all over his head, suppressing the flames from every horn on his large elongated head and overpowered him. Mephisto bellowed and cowered in the red shielded cage in the air.

Exclamations and gasps followed as the seven exquisite-looking diadems began to fall from the sky. Grimacing in agony, Mephisto cried out aloud, using his evil words of power, and immediately the diadems could be seen travelling through the air, as he writhed in pain. The young man cried out in a language, which sounded like the same language Gula had spoken over the golden egg and had caused it to open, "Aweata-afarfielda-magnatatikitata ephazaba ga." (Away to afar to the far place to Hephzibah the earthly keeper, go.) The crowd watched, as one by one, the diadems disappeared out of sight.

The rainbow-clad young man spoke again, "Commoteh," (Come before me,) and the angelic beings bowed before him, and then became the seven eagles once more. They circled in the air around him before flying back down to the earth and into the golden egg, which immediately closed up again. Then the egg and the protective shield around everyone on the ground vanished, and Mephisto and his minions were now being held in the air in a magnetic force field.

The crowd watched as the young man transformed and became the giant golden eagle once more. It flew over and picked up Trevor's lizard from off the tree branch with its giant beak.

"The eagle has got Trevor's Pinkie," cried Nikhil.

"Amazing miraculous works from those above," cried Eleanor.

"Mephisto and his minions were at work too," cried the strange young girl, although she sounded wounded.

"I do not believe that you have seen the end of my master."

"What work?" asked Eleanor, "That old fox has no power over good, except what we, through a lack of knowledge and belief give away to him," she said proudly.

All the cries, gasps and fear ceased. Everyone stood looking up, eager to see what would happen next.

"This is the work of the gods," said a woman from her side of the wooden fencing, which separated two gardens.

"What say you of the goddess," remarked Huldah, with a smile.

In a little while they noticed that the tabby was back in place on the branch of the treetop.

"Man!" cried Trevor, as the great golden eagle circled in the air and a brilliant rainbow trailed behind. It flew towards the tree again and, in a flash, the kitten was on the eagle's back. The giant magnificent bird manoeuvred in the air before flying down to the ground. This dazzled the people, causing them to close their eyes and gasped. But when they opened their eyes again, they saw that it was Carl who stood before them, holding a silver cage with the lizard safely inside it, and in his other hand, he held the kitten. He smiled and placed the kitten on the ground, and then he handed the cage to Trevor.

"Here is your Pinkie," he said, a broad smile lighting up his face.

"What's happened to the shadowy fiend, Mephisto?" asked Gula.

Tom, still excited replied, "I must admit, I was really scared when he became the dragon, and even more frightened, when he became that beastly humanoid."

"You heard Gula, that was Mephisto's true self, at least, what he has now become," said Nikhil.

"Yes, agreed Huldah, "a master of hideous disguises." The prophetess Huldah said her goodbyes and then disappeared before their very eyes in a ball of golden rays.

"And you Carl, em...." Nikhil looked in awe at his friend, he was unable to finish his sentence, but Gaia finished it for him.

"It was you, Carl," she said, "You became the giant golden eagle. You didn't die. Your sister and your mum said you wouldn't." Gaia looked completely enchanted in Carl's presence. Carl smiled down at her.

"He transformed into a big tall person the colour of the rainbow." Mary finished, looking even more amazed at Carl.

Nikhil noticing, grinned. "So, should we call you Rainbow Boy from now on, instead of Carl?" he asked.

"He's known by many names in the higher realms, but yes, today, above, he was Rainbow Morning Star," Gula told them. She had remembered what the old woman, who had transformed into an angelic being, had said, many years ago, while she was out walking with her parents and her brother one morning. The being had called her brother, Prince Wobniar, which means Rainbow.

Carl also remembered what was said to him too. 'There will come a time when you will remember who you were.' For now, his memory was not for him to share, but to cherish, and his powers are not to flaunt, but to be used for the highest greatest good of the earth and its inhabitants.

Tom laughed a little and tapped Carl on his shoulder. "So, what should it be my friend, a change of name, or..." Tom's delighted laughter stopped him from finishing his sentence.

"I hope I will always be Carl, to my friends," he replied, with a modest smile.

While the friends were busy making much of Carl, Mephisto had somehow managed to release himself and his minions from the magnetic forcefield because, in its place, they saw the dark Shadow in the air, travelling a great distance away, and a flock of crowbates following behind him. They watched as the Shadow and his crowbates changed into human-looking creatures and slowly descended downwards, into the earth, and disappear from sight.

The tabby meowed and Trevor looked at the lizard.

"My Pinkie," he cried in delight.

Carl turned and looked beyond the tree. The hedge was no longer glowing like fire, it was green once more.

Apart from Carl's friends, everyone else had walked out of the back gardens, still excited, until a strange white mist surrounded them for a few seconds. This cleared away their memories of what took place, and they began to talk normally and went about their everyday business. The remaining friends turned towards the spot where Carl had placed the tabby, but the kitten was gone.

Tom, Carl and Gula, looked at each other and smiled knowingly, before they joined the others in pretend search for the kitten, Clovis. They combed the immediate area, but they only disturbed several birds. The children watched the birds fly skywards, and then they heard the voice like that of the one from the burning bush:

"You all look as if you search for 'the cat among the pigeons.' Stop searching. Clovis is safely back where he is supposed to be, but only for a short while longer - Here me. It will soon be necessary for seven friends to journey to Hephzibah. The golden diadems must be retrieved and returned to the heavenly keeper. However, before that can be accomplished, Mephisto's deadly virus is growing and spreading rapidly. His intent is to infect and destroy the entire world and its population. It must be located. Be warned, only one has the power and authority to destroy this virus."

Carl and Gula knew that the voice was not referring to either of them, but listened intently with their friends, expecting to be told where to locate the virus, and which one among them would be able to destroy it, but they were greeted with silence. Most of them had looked at Carl, believing the voice spoke of him, but he shook his head, saying, "Don't look at me."

Craig shouted, "You are sending young kids on a fool's errand. Where is this deadly virus to be found, and why have you chosen children to do the task of adults?"

After a while longer the voice came again. "There is no need to shout. I can hear even your thoughts. Long ago the adults failed. Look to the land of Africa, deep in the deadliest jungle. One amongst you possesses the ability to guide you all safely, and that person will be your ultimate guide."

They turned to face Carl once more.

"You are all wrong," he told them, "I am not the one to look to."

Craig laughed.

Mary turned to Craig, and frowning she asked him, "Why do you laugh Craig, is it you?"

"Me!" responded Craig, with an angry stare. "No way! Do I look like a tour guide to you? I know as much about Africa as you, Mary Stuart, which is nothing."

The voice came again.

"Be warned, you will be distracted, forced to undertake a mission of mercy, and even someone dear to one among you, will also be taken. Be further warned, imminent danger and death threatens, but you will not be alone."

"I suppose you are expecting us to be grateful," whispered Trevor, in a sarcastic manner. They heard quiet laughter. They waited as before, but no further instructions or guidance came.

Looking surprised, they turned and looked to the east, west, north and south, to try and determine from which direction the voice had come. Carl and his sister, Gula, knew the voice, and so did their friend, Tom, because they had heard her before.

After saying their goodbyes, the friends parted company and went their separate ways home, each still mindful of what the voice had said about the near future, and each secretly wondering which, if any of them, will become one of the powerful seven.